Dundury

To Scott

Ava Lindsey Chambers

ALSO BY AVA LINDSEY CHAMBERS

STORIES FOR THE SPIRIT-FILLED
BELIEVER
"Ugly Cat"

O' GEORGIA
"The Box"

FROM THE HEART
STORIES OF LOVE & FRIENDSHIP
"How Great Is Love?"

SACRED STONES:
"One Smooth Stone"

Dundury

Ava Lindsey Chambers

FirstWorks Publishing Co., Inc.
Marietta, GA

Dundury

Copyright ©2004

Ava Lindsey Chambers

Published by FirstWorks Publishing Co., Inc.
firstworkspublishing.com

For information, please address:
FirstWorks Publishing Co., Inc.
P.O. Box 93
Marietta, GA 30061-0093

Photography and cover design created by
Audra Pettyjohn of Evolution Design
Dawsonville, Georgia

Library of Congress Control Number: 2004101824
ISBN: 0-9716158-2-9

Printed in the United States of America

For my parents, MarviLane and Julian Lindsey, who watch over me from Heaven. And to my husband, Russell, and our children, Rebecca, Sara, Luke, and Hanna, who are and always will be the loves of my life.

To my Mignon, whose loving arms cradled my youth and guided my future…

Prologue

"Bob, honey," Bertha said. "I've got something for you."

Bob lifted his head, expecting a birthday present. For two years he'd lived with Bertha; two years wondering when his mother would come get him. "What is it?"

"A letter from your mama."

"Is she coming home? Is she coming for my birthday?"

"No, child," Bertha said, stepping away from him. "She'll not come."

Bob grabbed the letter from her and ran out of the room. Tears of love streamed down Bertha's face. For the millionth time, she bowed her head, praying for the strength to guide him.

Bob bolted down the stairs and out to the backyard where he climbed the old mimosa tree. He struggled, fighting the brittle limbs as his fingers held tight to the envelope. The letter held a soft scent that wafted through his memory like a lullaby. Finally positioned in the middle of the tree, he ripped open the envelope and stared at the handwritten words:

My dearest child:

I had to leave you just before your tenth year. Forgive me, son. It was the only conceivable thing I could do for all of us. You will be safe with Bertha. She will instruct you so that you may fulfill your destiny. I may only guard you with my heart and hold you in my prayers. Never doubt the power we have been given. Father will guide you.

All my love,
Julia Kittendorf

Bob read her short note over and over again, but not one word of it had made any sense to him. He recognized her handwriting, yet the sound of her words was strange and mysterious, as if it were a cryptic message that he should have understood. He slowly moved his fingers over the words she had written. *Mother touched this page,* he thought, then brought the scented sheet to his lips. He pinched his eyes shut and tried not to cry.

"Why mother? Why?," he begged, fighting the anger boiling in the pit of his stomach that raced to be free. "What is a *destiny*," he said, touching the word she had written, and whispered, "You can't leave me, Mother... I love you... I need you."

"Bob, it's getting late," Bertha called out to him in a soft voice. "Come in now," she said, standing at the back door, wiping her hands in her apron. She took a deep breath. "It's time for your dinner."

"Yeah, I'm coming," he shouted. Anger fired his heart and he climbed down the tree and slowly meandered back to the house. He stopped for a moment; his fingers released their hold on the letter that drifted into the bowels of an old dead stump. "You keep it," he said, and a firefly fluttered up from the summer grass.

2001

Chapter 1

Bob glared at the phone on his desk. The ring pierced his senses. "You come in to be by yourself, maybe accomplish something and..." Another ring halted his muttering. "Just great!" he said, grabbing the phone. "Who is it?"

"A voice from your past."

Bob's eyes went wide with disbelief. "Davis?"

"Yeah," he laughed. "What's up?"

I haven't heard from you in over ten years and that's all you've got to say? He moved the phone to his other ear. "Where are you?" He came forward in his chair.

"Dundury."

"You've got to be kidding!" He felt the clamminess covering his hands.

"I'm not kidding, Bob. I'm really here. The town is even more beautiful than I remembered. The people are warm and there's this girl..."

"You can't stay there, Davis."

"C'mon! Surely you don't believe all the crap everyone pumped into us. I've inherited some property, finally got a clear title on it, and now I'm going to work my dream." Silence filled the moment until Davis continued. "It's time we put the past in its place. Can't you help me? I'm not asking much. I'm going to make this town a showplace. Publicity, that's the ticket! You can do that for me, Bob."

"We can't start this again, Davis. People *can't* go to Dundury."

"Get over it, Bob," he said, then started laughing. "People *have* been coming. The Inn is a bed and breakfast now. Couples have been getting married here."

"What... what have you done?"

"A little love in Dundury, Bob. It's a good thing! Do you remember Lisa?"

"Who?"

"Lisa Hardin...she lives in the Dundury mansion. She has Grace."

The receiver hit the blotter on his desk with a thud. *This can't be happening*, Bob thought. And yet, he knew he couldn't stop it. He had succeeded in putting Dundury out of his mind. Life was good--finally. He slowly wrapped his hand around the receiver. As if about to taste poison, he forced the words from his mouth. "I'll get in touch in a couple of days. Give me Lisa's phone number. I'll see what I can do."

"Great!" Davis said. "Lisa knows everything. It'll work. I just know it!"

"Sure." A slamming door drew Bob's attention. "I've gotta go," he said, then hung up the phone.

He looked up at the clock on the wall; it was Bertha, his secretary. He couldn't remember when Bertha had come into his life, but she was the closest thing to a mother he'd ever known. She worked as his secretary now, always encouraging him and tending to his every need.

"You're here before me? That's a switch," the hint of a

laugh punctuated her smile while her raised brows questioned him. "It's only seven thirty." She glanced to her wristwatch.

"Thought I'd catch up, but the phone hasn't stopped since I got here."

"Who's after you?" Bertha said, staring into his eyes.

"No one in particular," he said, returning her stare. *Why did you say that? Has Davis contacted you, too.* He sensed she was reading his mind, then focused his attention on the papers stacked on his desk. "Now you can handle the calls and I can get down to business."

"Do you need anything?"

"I'll let you know," he said as the closing door gave way to a sudden guilt. All the predictions came flooding back to him. *It was supposed to have been put to rest. What is Davis thinking? What's he been doing all these years? How long have you been in Dundury, Davis?* A flood of tears filled his gray, blue eyes. "I can't do this. I'm not the one," he whispered, his pleas ignored by the universe, as his head fell forward into his hands.

Bertha walked to her desk, opened the lower vacant drawer, and dropped her purse into its place. She feared her prayers had gone unanswered, that she'd become too complacent, too content, that her care and love had saved Bob. She knew that all she had feared these last twenty-five years was about to erupt, no matter how hard she begged the powers that be. "I've got to do something for that boy," she whispered, reaching for the phone on the corner of her desk.

"Oh, no..." Karen grumbled, grabbing the pillow and pulling it over her head.

"Hi! It's Karen," her answering machine announced. "That's right, I'm not here, so please leave your number."

"Miss Garrity, this is Bertha Jones...Bob's secretary."

Karen jumped out of bed. "Damn," she growled, tripping over her shoes. She reached the phone. "I'm here."

"I'm sorry to disturb you, Miss Garrity, Bob wants to see you."

"Why?"

"Well, he needs to see you today."

"*What?*" The old lady's irksome ways had bothered Karen for years. She plopped down on her bed, pushed the receiver closer to her ear as bittersweet memories reached back to long summer days.

She'd always felt left out. Bob and her brothers had spent hot afternoons playing baseball and taking delight in making fun of her poor attempts at swinging the bat. Picnic suppers in the back yard turned into overnight camp outs that never included her. Back then, Karen had thought Bertha was Bob's mother; it never occurred to her to ask why Bertha was black and Bob was white. No one ever mentioned the difference. It was accepted, as were all the strange rules that Bertha had enforced.

No one was ever allowed to enter Bob's house where candles gleamed eerily from every window. They only cradled the shadows and deepened her curiosity, until she'd sneak up to the house to peer into their world which had been off-limits and closed to her. And then, Bertha's face would glare back from the abyss.

"Karen?"

"I'm here, Bertha," she said, focusing on the present.

"Bob needs to see you--today."

"Why?"

"I really don't know, Karen. You'll just have to come in," Bertha said, holding the phone away from her lips; the lie made her nauseous.

"Okay," Karen said, fighting the irritation that began to build. Patience wasn't one of her virtues. "I'll be there as soon as possible."

"Do try to hurry, " Bertha said.

"Right," Karen said. She turned and squinted, trying to read the clock on her nightstand. "Not even eight o'clock," she muttered, staggering into the bathroom, and flipping on the switch for the light. "Why the urgency?" she asked her cat, then turned on the water faucets. "Well, Calico, guess I'll just have to go in and see what Bob wants." The cat yawned, stretched, and sauntered away as steam consumed the small space.

Wonder what made Bob need me? Her mind whirled, stimulated under fingers vigorously rubbing her scalp as the soapy water ran down her face. She stepped out of the shower, wrapping the towel around her, then stared in the mirror. *Is that old bird trying to set us up?* Her wet brown hair slapped her cheek as she bent over and pulled the blow dryer out of the cabinet. The hot air felt good on her face.

Satisfied, she pulled the half-wet mass into a ponytail, brushed the mascara wand through her lashes, then quickly dusted her cheeks with blush. Without thinking, she dabbed a little perfume behind each ear.

She stared into the mirror, then turned critical eyes to her thin waist. *I really should eat better. I look like a waif.* Her hazel eyes glared back with disdain. "Too fat, too thin, what does it matter," she asked her reflection.

"Okay, Calico," she said, hugging her little friend, "An adventure awaits--that is, *if* I can find my keys," she said, dropping the cat, and searching through the mounds of paper on her kitchen pass-through.

Then she heard the jingle of keys. "Calico!" she yelled out with a laugh, running back into the living room. "What are you sitting on?" Little paws lay across her key chain. "You little rascal," she said, grabbing the keys and heading for the door.

Karen cut through the early-morning city traffic along Peachtree Street, swung onto Tenth Street, and sailed through the green light that put her at the northbound ramp heading for Marietta. The interstate glowed with the headlights of the bumper-to-bumper commuters who made their slavish morning trek into Atlanta.

The drive to Marietta, unlike the southbound trip to Atlanta, afforded serenity in a way that seized upon so many memories of the town she had known as home. Its city square, surrounded by quaint little shoppes and cafes serving up culinary feasts, had emerged as a picture postcard. Marietta had always had its own distinctive charm that even progress couldn't expunge. Marietta remained, retaining its historic relevance from a time hellbent on destruction. Marietta managed to survive General Sherman's assault during the War Between The States.

Karen smiled when she reached *The Big Chicken*, the huge Kentucky Fried Chicken sign that had become a noteworthy landmark. *I didn't realize how much I'd missed you*, she silently told the big bird whose bill punched the morning sky. She turned onto Roswell Street that would bring her to the Marietta Square.

She drove once around the Square, then caught the light that put her on Cherokee Street heading north. The side street quickly came into view and she turned onto the narrow lane bordered by newly-renovated houses, though faithful to their original designs.

Bob's house came into view. The old place had always held a strange kind of appeal, perhaps it was the *shotgun* style of the house with its long hallway running from front to back; which gave credence to the timeworn tale that a shot fired from the front door could travel unobstructed straight through and out the back door.

Karen pulled into the side driveway, parked around back, and followed the shrub-lined walkway to the front door, hop-scotching from one-stepping stone to the next. She glanced up and smiled at the light winking from the second story window.

Dundury

Karen pushed open the front door, startled to be facing a steep staircase. A small door stood ajar along the side wall of the stairs. She stepped across the threshold as Bertha came from behind the open door.

"Here," Bertha said, handing Karen a candle. "Follow me."

Karen took the candle, shaking her head, and followed Bertha Jones up the stairs and into the outer office adorned with plants and candles. Each scent seemed to mix in perfection.

"I like the way you've done the place. I always wondered how you'd decorate the interior of a..."

"A home?" Bertha turned to Karen, her brow raised with that familiar hint of caution.

"Yes, as a matter of fact," Karen said, straightening her back. "Why was it always out of bounds?"

"I don't care for children running through my things."

"What about Bob? Weren't you like his Mammy?"

"That's an odd choice of words for this day and age," Bertha Jones said.

"I didn't mean it as an insult." Karen said, feeling Bertha's intimidating stare. "I just thought... I mean..."

"Maybe you should go in and see what he wants," Bertha said, pointing to the appropriate door.

Karen squared her shoulders and pushed open the door.

Bob looked up. "Morning, Karen. What's up?"

"*What's up?*" She perched her hands on her hips. "Bertha told me to hurry over here."

"She did?" He cleared his throat. *Bertha... what have you done?*

"Yes, she did. Didn't you know? She acted like you had some emergency. Called me at the crack of dawn."

Bob felt the beads of perspiration popping out on his forehead. "Oh, come on. It couldn't have been that early. You always were a sleepy head."

"Don't change the subject. What did you want?"

"You know she doesn't like you calling her Bertha."

"Okay, fine." Karen blew out the candle in her hand, as well as the one on the corner of his desk." She switched on the lamp. "What's this thing you and Bertha have with candles?"

"Candles make warmth and light and dispel the darkness and..."

"Will you please stop rambling!"

He hung his head.

"Well?"

"There's this town called Dundury."

"So?"

"It's a strange town," he said, looking up at her. "I have a friend there, he's got a place there."

"And?" she said impatiently.

"It's a bed and breakfast."

"So?"

"I was complaining to Bertha about not having the time to go down," he said, standing and coming around his desk. He sat on the corner, beside Karen. "You know, I'm trying to get the magazine going."

"Yes. *Highways and Bi-ways of the South*, you told me that." Suddenly, her eyes went wide. "You want me to do a story!"

"I told him I'd help, but it's just not possible."

"I can help you." She smiled. "I can use a little time off and," her smile was full blown. "I'd love to have you print something I've written."

"We can't pay you much. You'd have to take pictures with your own camera and buy your own film." *I can't let her go*, he warned himself.

"That's okay."

"No," Bob said, shaking his head. "I don't think it'll work."

They stood silent, staring at one another. He felt as if he

were a kid again. He remembered one weekend, when he was about fifteen, and Karen--well, she couldn't have been more than twelve. Her brothers had gone out of town. She came over to his house and, somehow, she'd convinced him to help her learn how to play ball. He'd spent hours trying to teach her how to swing a bat. That was the day he realized that he was actually quite fond of her; that in his own way he loved her and that love would never die. They had talked late into the evening and she had confided her secret dreams to him.

"Bob?" Karen said, leaning closer to him. "Remember when we were kids?"

"Yes," he said. "I remember how determined you always were. You want the assignment? Fine, go to Dundury." *I should warn her.* His mind was a jumble. *Don't send her,* he told himself. *Why did you choose her, Bertha?*

"When do I leave," she asked, sliding off the desk.

"This afternoon," he said, feeling his heart missing a beat.

Karen headed for the door. "I need to make arrangements for my cat," she said.

Bertha Jones looked up as Karen stepped into the reception area. Old papers and photos littered the top of her desk. "Are you going, Miss Lewis?"

"Yes, and you'll have to call me with directions to Dundury. I've got to find a place for my cat."

"Good," Bertha said, trying to hide her satisfaction. *Yes, girl, you're the one. You can do it.* "I'll have a courier drop off the information you'll need."

"That will be fine," Karen answered.

Bertha Jones followed Karen down the stairs. "I could have someone look after your cat," she said, not waiting for an answer, and disappeared behind the little door.

"That's not necessary." Karen yelled out.

A man in a dark coat threw open the front door and pushed past Karen. He lumbered up the stairs, three at a time, staring down at her as he made his ascent. The coldness that clung to him should have touched her; she was oblivious to it.

The man, reaching the second floor, went directly to Bob's door and flung it open. Purpose filled every step as he crossed the thresh-hold. "You've done it," his heavy voice said.

Shock fired Bob's eyes as the color evaporated from his face.

"I will stop the cycle this time," The voice rumbled low, like the warning growl of a tiger.

"There's nothing to stop." *He can't know. He can't know,* Bob told himself over and over.

The man slammed his hands down on the desk, supporting his weight as he leaned over into Bob's face. "Don't lie to me," he said. "It's begun again. The signs are all in place."

Bob forced his legs to stand. "Is that why you're here?"

"I've been watching you your whole life, Bob."

"Like a good *father*," Bob said, cautiously making his way around the desk in an effort to stand tall and defiant. "I hate that we share the Kittendorf name."

His father almost smiled. "If you try to leave town, I'll know it."

"I'm not leaving." Bob said, pointing to his desk. "Look at all this work."

"Work? You've known the work for which your life was really meant." A cold hate filled his father's eyes. Then, the older Kittendorf turned and left.

It was beginning again and it had to be stopped-- too many generations were at risk.

Dundury

Chapter 2

Karen drove down the empty, flat roads through middle Georgia. She thought she understood the directions Bertha had sent. She pulled onto the shoulder of the road and searched the glove box for the map.

"The damn town isn't even listed." she said, then punched the button on the air conditioning panel. "And, it's hot!" she yelled, positioning the vents so they'd blow directly on her face.

She lifted the cup of iced tea out of the holder and pulled back onto the highway. "Oh, great--it's turned to lukewarm water," she said, pushing the cup back in its holder as she pressed the gas peddle to the floor. "Okay, Bertha, where's the damn town? Oh, excuse me! She doesn't like to be called Bertha," Karen said, then slapped her forehead in a reprimand. "And, dammit--who the hell am I going to interview, Bertha? You never gave me the guy's name!"

"Damn!" she shouted, swerving around a possum that ran into the road." And there, looming right in front of her, was a road sign welcoming her to Dundury.

A red sports car came flying out of nowhere, just inches from her front bumper. Karen pumped the brakes as she frantically downshifted, fighting to hold the car on the road. Anger flew far outside the realm of reason. Everything from lipstick to a muggy cup of tea slid off the dashboard and into her lap.

"You damned idiot!" she screamed, pounding her horn. Only the need to keep both hands on the wheel kept her from lifting her finger.

A red light stopped both cars. Karen jumped out screaming at the top of her lungs. "Are you insane--or is it a death wish?" Red-faced and panting, she was ready for battle.

Long legs slowly emerged from the little roadster. The tights that encased them were decorated with dragons and fairies. Pink tipped fingernails drew her eyes to slim fingers that pushed the door open.

Karen looked into the woman's face. "Lisa--Lisa Hardin!"

The lanky lass looked surprised as she slowly walked toward her. She threw her arms around Karen. "Bob said you were coming."

Karen stepped back. "You know Bob?"

"Yes," she said, looking Karen over. "Are you okay?"

"I guess, except for some long lost *pal* nearly killing me. I was ready to take your head off," Karen said. "I thought I recognized those tights. I can't believe you're still dressing like that."

Lisa rolled her eyes. "So, I hear you have an assignment."

Karen frowned a puzzled look.

"You're going to like Davis Hamilton, the owner of the Inn, and you don't need to stay there. Save the expense and stay here, with me," Lisa said.

Karen hesitated, *she knows his name.* "Yes, the Inn is probably expensive." *Or was it Bob's idea to stay with Lisa?* "I wouldn't want to be a bother. What about your family?"

Lisa shrugged. "No family," she stuttered. "None of that--

just me and, um." The pause was long enough to pique Karen's curiosity. "Just me," Lisa said, forcing a smile.

"Well, okay, if you think you can stand me," Karen said. "You do have a lot to tell me, like: why are you here? How do you know Bob?"

"You haven't changed," Lisa said, toying with her keys. "Follow me. You're going to love our little town. You might even find your heart's desire here."

A good story is all I want, Karen told herself as she got back into her car to follow Lisa. "Okay, Lisa, you were a little too obvious when you ignored my question about Bob." The scenery of huge oak trees overhanging the road and, old homes peeping from behind branches that twisted and turned, quelled her curiosity.

Gnarly limbs pointed the way as she followed Lisa. "What stories could you tell," Karen asked the mighty oak. It seemed as if history oozed from behind every tree. Won*der how that damn Yankee Sherman missed burning this town on his March To The Sea?* This many antebellum homes didn't exist anywhere else in Georgia... *so why isn't it on any map?*

Karen gasped when Lisa pulled into the driveway of the stateliest mansion thus far; it's beauty was breathtaking. Six Doric columns supported a porch polished with time. Massive ferns overhung stands that sat perched between each of the columns. The paint was perfect. Not one cobweb claimed a corner. Every well-kept inch of the house spoke of time immortal.

"Are you sure you're okay?" Lisa asked as she banged on the driver's window.

"I'm fine. Just a little overwhelmed."

"Well, come on in and take a load off," Lisa said, walking along the drive to the side of the old mansion.

Karen grabbed her purse and slid off the car seat. She followed Lisa through the side door that opened into a massive kitchen where huge floor-to-ceiling cabinets filled one entire wall. A spinning wheel surrounded by crockery graced a corner, while a smooth stone hearth sported a collection of iron skillets with the mantle above displaying a trove of stove lifters.

"Everything here is so old." Karen said, glancing to the far wall and the most impressive feature so far, a glass cabinet filled with glistening china and delicate crystal. Refractions of light danced off the dishes like rainbows glittering off a still mountain lake. "Wow! This is incredible. You must entertain a lot."

"Not anymore. My grandmother used all this stuff. I hold the Historical Society meetings here once in a while, but I just can't seem to manage the same elegance."

"I've never seen such pieces. They must be worth a fortune," Karen said. "I can only imagine what the rest of the house looks like."

Lisa smiled. "It's just an old family home. I moved back after school and got a job teaching third graders at the elementary school."

The story seemed odd. They had hung around together during college, yet Karen hadn't known Lisa all that well, and she'd never heard a thing about Lisa being from such a wealthy Southern family. Stuff like that was always tailor made for gossip.

"Who was your roommate at Georgia?" Karen asked.

"I lived alone in the dorm, then I rented a little trailer. You remember, the one behind the doctor's office."

"The doctor's office was a refurbished antebellum house, wasn't it?" Karen asked, lost in the fineries that filled the room.

"Well, yeah, sort of," Lisa said.

The gracious smile and perfect manners signaled a congenial hostess; Karen wondered, *Maybe there is a story here.*

Lisa reached for the brass pulls on the heavy mahogany double pocket doors that opened to the foyer. They walked down the long polished hallway and in the middle of the living room floor sat the most beautiful little dollhouse that Karen had ever seen. "Oh, Lisa, this is darling! Where did it come from?"

"My great-grandfather made it."

Karen stepped closer. "It's this house, isn't it?"

"Well, almost. It's what the original house looked like. There have been a few changes over the years." Karen knelt down to the replica and Lisa drew a quick breath.

"Don't get too close. It's very fragile," she said in a voice that took on a higher pitch as she grabbed Karen's hand. "You must not."

"I'm sorry. I just wanted to see inside. How'd you get all the stuff in there? Was it put in before the fourth wall was built," she said, reaching for the roof.

"Get away!" Lisa screamed.

"I'm sorry," she said, pulling her hand back. "If it's so fragile, why don't you move it--it is dead center in the middle of the floor, Lisa."

"It can't be moved. Just stay away from it and all the others you see. People around here get upset about their houses. It's a status symbol."

"There are *more* like this one?"

"Well, not exactly like this one. All the old homes in Dundury have their own."

"Does the Inn have one?"

"Yes, of course. Now, come upstairs."

Karen obeyed. She paused at the top of the stairs and looked back down on the little house. She blinked her eyes, doubting that she actually saw tiny lights glowing inside the replica. *What's going on here*, she thought. *And, why did Bob contact Lisa?*

"Here we are," Lisa said. "This room should do nicely," she said wiggling her nose. "I'm sorry, it smells a little musty." She went to the heavy brocade drapes, slid them along the brass pole, and lifted the window. A cool breeze fluttered in. "There weren't any closets when the house was originally built, so you can hang your clothes in that wardrobe over there. I'll take a few things out so you'll have some room."

Karen nodded and pointed across the room. "How do you mount that bed?"

Laughter spilled out of Lisa. "I know it's awfully high, but there's a step stool underneath, and you'll feel like a queen when you get up there."

Karen turned, examining the rest of the room. In addition to the wardrobe, a mirrored chest sat in one corner, a pitcher and a towel rested on top. As the sun streamed in, lighting the knotty pine paneled walls, Karen could almost imagine faces peering at her. The room glowed an inviting warmth. "It's like stepping into the past."

"Try out the bed," Lisa said, motioning to her. "I'll go and get your things."

Karen knelt down and reached for the stool, the frayed dust ruffle tickled her fingers. She climbed the three steps up to the mattress and slowly lowered herself. It felt as if it grabbed and pulled her into its feathered down, the ticking overwhelming her senses as sleep overpowered her.

Hours later, Karen stretched and sat up. The drapes had been closed, erasing the sunlight. The faint sound of footsteps drummed in her head, and then, a gentle knock sounded at the door.

"Good Morning," Lisa said. "I brought you breakfast or, maybe I should say, brunch, you sleepyhead!" Lisa placed the tray on the bedside table, lifted the napkin and turned to Karen..

"What time is it?"

"About eleven-thirty, I think."

"Good grief! I've got to set up that interview."

"It's done." A conspirator's grin lighted Lisa's face.

Karen covered her yawn.

Lisa climbed the steps up to the bed and landed with a bounce that jostled the two of them. "There's a historical meeting today. A very special one. I think I've got something you can wear. You're going to be my honored guest. You'll meet tons of people."

"Wait. Slow down."

"I told you about the meetings..." Lisa said, looking about the bed as if searching for something.

"And?"

"Well, it's at the Inn. Isn't that great?" She slid off the bed and headed for the door. "Your dress is almost ready. The bath is at the end of the hall."

With that, the door closed. Karen shook her head; the confusion remained. "A dress I can wear? Does she think I didn't bring a dress?" she questioned, looking around the room.

The smell of bacon drew her eyes to the tray where fat blueberries popped from sugar topped muffins. An array of fruit colored the plate next to a small china pot that matched the vase. The display was beautiful. "Hope there's coffee in that pot." Disappointed to find only weak tea, Karen munched on the bacon, then the fruit. She giggled to herself, wondering how long it had been since anything this healthy had crossed her lips.

"Knock, knock. It's me again," Lisa said, opening the door. "Here's your dress!"

Karen sat speechless, staring at the silken dream. A fitted green bodice flowed into an enormous skirt that shimmered as if illuminated from a hidden source, its low-scooped neckline begging for jewels. Lisa smiled, dragging in a magnificent hoop made of whale boning. She wrestled with the hoop that resisted, finally falling to the floor.

"I'm a little worried about the shoes," she said, tossing the hoop onto the bed. "I had no idea what size you wear. Most of the shoes are rather small. I have to custom order mine. Guess I'd look funny with small feet, though, especially being so tall."

"I wear a size six," Karen said.

Lisa pulled back the covers and inspected Karen's feet. "Thank goodness. I was so worried. I didn't know what to do about size, though color could have been a problem too, and..."

Lisa's penchant for chatter was beginning to wear thin. Karen couldn't figure out what had happened to Lisa and why she chose to live such an existence. When the summer break was over and dress-up time at an end, she wondered what type of woman could shift gears to return to a room full of third graders.

"The meeting is at two," Lisa jabbered. "Bath is down the hall. Oh, and, I'll bring you the shoes," she said, one hand tucked under her chin as she waved with the other. It was a most disturbing gesture.

Karen quickly gulped the last of her bacon, then raced down the hall. Inside the bathroom sat a footed, white porcelain bathtub that took forever to fill. The bottle of lavender oil intrigued her and she spilled a bit into the tub, then eased herself down. The water rose deep around her while the soothing lavender scent enveloped her. "Perfect," she said, until the sound of footsteps interrupted her repose.

"We really must hurry," Lisa called out from the hall.

Karen stood up and yanked the thick terry robe off the hook on the back of the door. Once belted, she opened the door and forced a pleasant smile.

"I won't let you make me late," Lisa pouted. "I woke you in plenty of time. What will the others think if we're late? It'll take forever to get you into your corset," Lisa said, pushing Karen down the hall and back into her room.

"A *what*?"

"You wear it under your gown. Now come on!" Lisa said,

lifting the corset and the dimity piece off the bed and holding it out in front of her, waiting for Karen to turn around.

"It looks like a torture device!"

"Put this on first," she said, handing Karen the cotton camisole.

Karen obeyed and smoothed the fabric around her waist.

Lisa grabbed Karen's arm and spun her around. "Here," she said, holding the corset lined with whale bone stays, and proceeded to wrap it around Karen's midriff. She jerked her around, threaded the laces through the eyelets, then pulled the lace ties as tight as she could.

"Are you wearing one of these things," Karen managed to say through a gasp.

"Yes, and you've got to help me with mine. I usually have to go without a corset 'cause I can't put it on by myself. But today," she smiled, turning Karen back around to face her. "Today, I'll be dressed to perfection."

"I can't breathe," Karen whined. "I can't wear this."

"You can--and you will," Lisa said, anger flashing from her eyes. And then, suddenly, a quiet consumed her.

Karen followed Lisa down the stairs. The sight of the little house basking in the afternoon sun beckoned her. She could almost imagine someone living inside.

"Come on, we'll never make it if you don't hurry! I don't want to arrive glowing."

"*Glowing?*"

"Yes. You know, pig's sweat. Men perspire... ladies glow."

For years, Karen had fought that unconscious, unsightly habit of twisting her mouth and wrinkling her nose in disgust. At this precise moment, her long fight was officially over. "And why would we *glow?*"

"Because we're walking."

"You've got to be kidding! In this get-up?"

"*Get-up*? I beg your pardon." Lisa's brows drew close.

"How far is it?" Karen asked.

"A few blocks."

Silence fell as heavy as the heat around the two women. Karen tried to pull in quick puffs of air, forcing them in and out of her lungs. She fought lightheadedness, hoping to stay calm enough to keep from hyperventilating. She began to wonder what punishment she would suffer if, by chance, she were *glowing* when they arrived at the Inn. "Lisa?"

Lisa ignored her, stepping up their pace.

A small purse hung from Karen's wrist. "I hope there's smelling salts in that bag," she yelled out.

Finally, Lisa stopped and turned around to Karen. "We're here. Stand up straight. Smile," she said, primping Karen's hair. "I'll make a lot of introductions. Try to pay attention and remember names." Lisa grabbed her elbow, pulling and guiding her through the ten-foot-high double doors. "Walk with me. We'll go all the way through the house and into the garden in the back."

"But, I..."

Lisa ignored her questions. Arriving at the rear of the Inn, she proceeded down the stone archway and opened the gate. She stepped onto the marble pentagon-shaped stones, defining the path that led to the trellis draped with roses, and the magnificent garden beyond. Women dressed in Civil War finery punctuated the grounds. Each offered a nod and a worried smile to Lisa as Karen followed, like a good puppet.

Karen broke away from Lisa and headed for the linen-topped tables under the trellis. She marveled at the display. Tables with crystal vases holding miniature red roses and gold-rimmed dishes designating each place setting decked the tables, while chilled crystal goblets *glowed* under the summer sun. The chairs at the tables were positioned far enough apart, allowing for the ladies' broad hooped skirts. Karen took the seat to the left of the only man in attendance.

Across from her sat a tiny woman, whose headful of tightly wrapped curls, reminded Karen of Margaret Mitchell's Aunt Pitty Pat from *Gone With The Wind*. Deep red lipstick filled an unusually small mouth. She winked at Karen and nodded to the gentleman beside her. Then, the woman began a curious exercise, taking her right index finger and outlining each finger on her left hand. Up and over, up and over the old woman performed her tedious task, which transfixed Karen's gaze. Then, the woman tugged slightly on each gloved finger, briskly rubbed the palms of her hands together, and slowly pulled the left glove off. She repeated the procedure for her right gloved hand. The gentleman nodded his approval.

A sudden uneasiness settled on Karen and she began searching for Lisa. The chiming of a spoon tapping crystal drew her attention. At the far end of the table, sitting as if the grand dame of the affair, Lisa waited. There wasn't a sound in the garden; even the robin perched on the gate dared not sing. An almost imperceptible nod from the gentleman was the cue to begin.

"Ladies, and our dear gentleman, at precisely two p.m., let us take note that our meeting began with the pouring of red wine," a voice in the crowd announced.

It seemed strange to Karen that the glasses were suddenly filled with wine. Wherever the servants had come from, they had disappeared just as mysteriously. Karen tried to stand, intent on breaking the bizarre mood of madness. Something pinned her dress to the ground. *Okay*, she thought, *I'm thirsy*. She reached for her glass. A shot of electricity flew from her fingertips and up to her elbow. The gentleman had laid his hand upon hers. Silence thickened between them.

Pale and relinquishing her grace, Lisa stared at Karen. Words stumbled out of her mouth; no one responded. Plates of salad appeared and ladies demurely placed their linen napkins on their laps.

The gentleman's hold remained tight.

"Either let go or--" she whispered, leaning into his ear. "Or, tell me your name."

"Davis," he whispered back and released his hold.

Okay, so you're the one I'm supposed to interview. Karen opened her napkin and let it float onto her lap. She sliced into the large lettuce leaves on her plate and pierced a small piece with her fork. No one else had dared take a bite. She refused to allow them to make her feel awkward. A sip of wine, which proved to be delicious, buoyed her courage.

She straightened her back and turned to Davis. "Salad not to your liking, *Mister* Hamilton?"

He smiled a sheepish grin. "I believe your friend is about to announce a toast--" he said, then paused and pointed down the length of the table, "To you."

"My friend," Karen gestured with her fork to Lisa who slumped into her chair, "has already taken her seat," she said as Lisa stared her down.

"I guess she'll forego the toast since you've already begun your meal," he said, flashing a sarcastic smile at Lisa who continued her stare in their direction.

Without any forethought or even knowing why, Karen pushed herself back from the table and stood up. "Ladies," she said. "Please enjoy your meal." She sat back down without so much as another word.

In unison, the women lifted their forks and jabbed at tiny bits of food that a mouse would have ignored. Karen, on the other hand, ate with gusto, glancing to the uneaten food on their plates. *What a waste all this is,* she told herself. The ladies, dressed in their favorite period costumes, reflected a time of trial and courage which reminded her that those long-ago times were filled with thriftiness and making-do. Something touched her leg. She felt it through the layers of heavy skirting.

"You require something," Karen said, turning to the Davis

Hamilton, who had yet to be formally introduced.

"Yes, I do require something," he responded.

Davis was beautiful, his tanned skin radiated with life. His manicured fingers completed the perfection of his attire. Karen imagined a cigar tucked inside a gold case in a vest pocket. His thicket of sandy blonde hair was impeccably styled, and his smile so manufactured that it could have been painted on. She felt his enigmatic air of sophistication, and arrogance. It was unmistakable, even charming in a way that surprised her.

"And, what is it you require?" Karen asked.

"You."

She felt a chill moving through her. Such attention from Davis would have made any other woman swoon, but she perceived a threat. She looked into his eyes, so dark as to be coal black, and almost impenetrable. She refused his intimidating game. "I beg your pardon."

"I require *you.*"

There was no mistaking his menacing tone. "I'm afraid you're just not my type," she said, managing as much politeness as she could muster, then lifted the crystal glass and gulped the last of her wine. Out of the periphery of her eye she saw Lisa standing at the end of the table.

"I want to introduce ya'll to my friend, Karen." A wave of heads gracefully turned toward her. "It is our hope that she will soon join us." Excited giggles filled the garden.

Several ladies stood up, came to Karen, and patted her shoulder. Some winked in her direction. One lady handed her a list of names and addresses and politely commanded her to call upon them as soon as convenient.

The late afternoon heat took its toll as well as the wine; its obliging catalyst--and suddenly everything faded to black.

Karen slowly opened her eyes, gazing up to the ceiling. A heavy-headed sense of dread took hold of her. *How the hell did I get back here?* She was back in her bedroom. "Lisa!"

"I'm here," Lisa said., opening the door and coming to the side of the bed.

"What happened to me... All I remember is all those women..." she said, grabbing hold of Lisa's hand.

"Just rest," Lisa said, patting her shoulder. "I think you drank too much wine?"

"He must have drugged me," she said, closing her eyes.

Chapter 3

"Oh, my head," Karen said, rubbing at her temples. Never in all her life had she felt so miserable. A stabbing pain throbbed in her head, making it nearly impossible to sit up.

"Awake, I see," the irritating voice said to her.

"How long have I been out of it?"

"Oh, a couple of days. Must have been the flu," she said nonchalantly.

"It's not flu season," Karen snapped, trying to sit up. "What are you people doing to me?"

Lisa laughed as she fluffed the pillows behind Karen's head. "You're being a bit paranoid, don't you think?" she asked, turning for the tray of food. "Maybe you had a bug before you came here. We certainly haven't done anything to you."

"I feel so weak and confused."

"You've had a fever, I think."

Karen looked into Lisa's eyes. "Have *you* been sick?"

"I'm never sick. Now, eat something," Lisa said, steadying the tray on Karen's legs as she straightened the coverlet.

The food would probably help my head, Karen reasoned. She didn't trust it, yet she couldn't starve either. "Have I been in this bed for two days?"

"Yes, and you'll be here a bit longer," Lisa said firmly.

"But..."

"Eat," Lisa commanded, then turned and left the room.

Two more days passed before Lisa agreed to Karen's demands to take a bath. Amazed at how weak she still was, Karen almost gave in to Lisa's suggestions to bathe her. Still, privacy would allow for the opportunity to devise a plan of escape. She felt every bit the prisoner. She impatiently waited while Lisa filled the tub, checking to make sure the water wasn't too hot.

"Can you get in by yourself?" Lisa asked through a smile, standing at the door.

"Yes, I think so," Karen said. "I'll be fine. I'll yell if I need you." After Lisa closed the door, Karen slid into the warmth of the tub and closed her eyes. *I've got to get out of here,* she thought, only momentarily contemplating whether she were crazy or just imagining the strange events and circumstances that overtook her. Weak arms slowly pulled a soapy rag across her body. *I'll call Bob,* she decided, splashing the warm water onto her face.

Karen staggered back down the hall to her room where she found clean pink pajamas folded neatly at the foot of the bed. Pulling them on exhausted her as did the weakness and the foggy recollections and non-answered questions.

She mounted the three steps and waged a small war with the down of the bed as she rolled to her back. She lay staring at the bedside table and the silver tray overburdened with sandwiches and fruit.

"I can't stand eating in this room," she told herself, rubbing her neck, and fearing the confusion that seemed unending. She stared at the ceiling. *The house is so still... Maybe Lisa went out,* she thought, and slowly slid her legs over the soft edge of the bed. Her feet slammed the floor with a thud that buckled her knees. "Where's the damn stool," she said, sitting on the floor.

"You curse far too much for a lady." An eerie voice wafted through the room.

She stood up; the quiet persisted. She grabbed her robe and opened the bedroom door. The hall had never looked longer. Framed faces glared down at her from the near-darkened walls. Each seeming to know a secret, one she was going to discover.

Where to start? Where to start? The cadence filled her as she slowly put one foot in front of the other and crept down the stairs, into darkness that swallowed everything.

This is great! How in the world am I going to find my way around? She moved like a blind person, until she kicked something. "The house," she whispered. She looked down and saw the hint of light coming from within it. She knelt down peeking through the tiny window. *Is someone there?*

Another pop of light flashed in the little house. Karen stretched out on her stomach and looked into the bottom floor. It was the same as the room in which she now lay. *Something's moving in there.* More light appeared and she saw the tiny switchplate on the wall. Karen stood up, moving to the same wall as in the tiny house feeling for the switch. Finding it, she flipped it on, flooding the room with soft light.

Curiosity consumed all caution. Without a second thought, she went back to the little house and began tugging and pulling on the roof. A fingernail tore off, its pain intensifying her determination, and she yanked on the roof. It gave way, splintering shards that sliced the palm of her right hand. She stood aghast to the sight of the little bedroom--the *same* bedroom in which she had slept.

A tiny doll lay asleep on the bed. *Poor thing, she doesn't get a stool, either,* she thought.

Her eyes traveled down the hall to the little bathroom

where she saw a terry cloth robe hanging on the door, along with matching towels--as the ones she had just used. "Now that's a little anal." Just as she was contemplating how to get a better look at the bottom floor, something darted across the bedroom floor.

Without hesitation she reached in and grabbed it. "My God! Are you real?" she whispered to the miniature woman wiggling in her hand. She was slim with long gray hair that hung to her waist. She was wearing pink pajamas and felt warm and delicate to the touch.

"You feel alive," Karen whispered to the little woman, remembering something she had read, about reindeer fur being used to stuff toys. The fur made the toy *warm up* when it made contact with body heat, as when a child hugs a toy. But, nobody could hug this toy. Karen turned it over.

"You're not even as long as my hand. What makes you move?" Karen continued to inspect the figure until she heard noises.

"What have you done!" Lisa screamed. "Are you crazy," she shrieked. "I told you not to touch the house! Dear God! You've broken the roof and... No! Oh, no!" Lisa screamed, lunging at Karen. In that moment a sickening splat echoed throughout the room.

Karen looked to the floor. A thin line of crimson-colored liquid ran down the delicate face to the edge of her tiny chin. The little lady's legs were bent at odd angles and her pajama top was ripped.

"You've killed her!" Lisa screamed, her nostrils flaring. Karen saw hate so intense that, if Lisa could, she would have committed murder in that fleeting moment.

"Get a grip, Lisa. It's a toy!"

"Are you blind--or some sort of idiot? She's *not* a toy!" Fat tears streamed down her face. "She's the last one we have."

"She's not a toy?" Karen asked in total disbelief.

Lisa knelt down to the broken little figure, "What will we all do now?" Reverently, she lifted the tiny woman and gently placed her on the miniature bed. Wiping away her tears, she said. "Mignon will know what to do."

"Who's Mignon?"

"I have to get Mignon," Lisa said, and raced out the front door.

Karen sank back to her knees. Slowly she lifted what she prayed could not possibly have been a living being. It was limp and when she turned it over, blood seeped from its wee mouth.

Karen began to shake, rocking back and forth, trapped in the horror of what she had done.

"This can't be! A toy doesn't bleed," She screamed. *People...real people...aren't this size.* "But, you're so frail, so precious. I didn't mean to drop you." *Damn, She's got me talking to a doll!*

The shrill ring of the phone jolted her. She staggered toward the sound and picked up the receiver. "Hello," she answered hoarsely.

"Karen? I've been calling for days. What's been happening down there?"

"Bob... Oh, Bob, I've killed her!"

"What's happened, Karen?"

"Lisa says she's real--she looks real and feels real... Oh, God! I killed her!"

"*Who* did you kill?"

"The little woman!"

"Grace?"

"Yes. I dropped her."

"Calm down, Karen. Let me talk to Lisa," Bob said, rubbing his neck, trying to focus as he paced behind his desk. *Shit, I knew something like this would happen.*

"She went out to call someone."

"Where's Grace?"

"Who?"

"The little one in the house."

"In my hand."

"*What*?"

"She's in my hand. The little woman is in my hand. Her little pink pajama shirt is ripped. Maybe I should look in the closet and see if she has any more clothes."

"Where did Lisa go, Karen?"

"I don't know..." she said, hanging up and looking at the miniature woman lying dead in her hand. "You're a doll! You're not real," she screamed, fighting reality.

Blood seeping from the tiny lips, warmed the palm of Karen's hand, and then, she saw her own injury. "I should wash my hands." Unwilling to put the woman down, she curled her fingers around the pocket-sized being, and started for the stairs.

"Get the humidor," said a curiously accented voice. It was a low and raspy, a voice filled with great authority. "She must be kept safe."

Karen whirled around. A huge woman, the color of caramel, wearing a long, purple robe, stood in the doorway. She slowly and gracefully stepped into the room, much like an ancient queen. "I know when trouble comes," she said, answering Karen's unasked question. "There will be more. Now, get the humidor."

"Where?"

"It's somewhere in this room."

A humidor...didn't men keep cigars in them? Fear paralyzed Karen as she stared at her hand.

"Give her to me, then," the woman said.

"No!"

"You can't help her," the queenly woman reassured her. "Give her to me."

"Who are you?" Karen asked.

"I am Mignon. Lisa summoned me."

"Why?"

"Because I have cared for them. Hand her to me."

"You don't even know her name."

"Do you?" the woman challenged.

A strange feeling seized hold of her heart. Yes, she did know her name. Bob had said it. She uncurled her fingers and looked down into the little face. It was worn and tired and much too familiar. "Her name is Grace."

"Yes, child." The huge robed woman said, taking a step closer. "What more does your heart see?"

"Grace wanted to die years ago. She's been so tired of waiting." Another step alerted Karen. "Get back!"

"I am to tend her."

Karen glanced around the room. "Where's Lisa?"

"Other folks had to be told."

"Who else?" Suddenly the words and their meaning hit her. There had been a murder, unintentional though it might have been, but a life was taken. A strange, beautiful little life had ended at her hands. *Lisa said she was the last one.*

"More will come," Mignon said, challenging Lisa's assertion.

"How?"

"Shhh! It cannot be told."

"Where did Grace came from?"

"There were many...in the old country, England 'tis said." Mignon touched a finger to her chin. "Ireland, maybe," she said, taking a step closer. "Maybe they came from a place we have all forgotten."

"She's the last in the world?" Karen asked with alarm.

"No, child, I pray not. We got to keep believing. More *must* come or the world will lose its order."

This isn't real. Karen shook her head, trying to free the fuzz that was intent on muddling her thoughts.

"'Tis as real as love," Mignon said and pointed. "Look, there in your hand. There's no denying what has happened."

The little one was beginning to lose her warmth. "I need to dress her before she is too stiff," Mignon said, kneeling down to the dollhouse, while inching closer to Karen.

"Do you think there are clothes in the closet?"

Mignon's nod was Karen's okay to turn the tiny doorknob.

A gasp, stifled by a sob, rushed from Karen's lips. "It's the gown--the one Lisa made me wear to the luncheon. I can't put that on her. I can't!"

"It's meant to be, child," Mignon said.

Believing nothing worse could happen, it did. Davis flung open the door.

He quickly surveyed the room, then frowned. "Where's Grace?" he demanded, moving straight for Karen. "You got too curious. Had to have a look," he snarled, seeing the condition of the roof on the little house. He glared at Mignon. "Where is Grace?"

"I have her," Karen said, unclenching her fingers. "She's getting cold."

Davis' face went white while his eyes blazed like black sparking coals. "Why so much blood on her clothes?"

"She killed her," Lisa said, rushing into the room and running to Davis' side.

"No, I didn't! I picked her up and then Lisa pushed me... and Grace fell."

"You killed her!" Lisa said, positioning herself between Davis and Mignon.

"Stop!" Davis hissed. "We must carry out her last wishes."

Karen maintained her gentle hold on the little body. *Why doesn't my hand hurt when I hold her?*

"Child," Mignon pleaded, "I must get her ready. I need the humidor."

Davis jerked his chin toward Karen. "She knows too much already, Mignon."

"Yes, and she deserves to know the rest.. It will help her let go."

"I won't let you do anything to her," Karen said, slowly backing away from the three.

Mignon, grabbed Davis' arm. "Show her the humidor."

Karen suddenly turned and raced for the door.

"Stop!" Lisa screamed.

Karen stopped. "The house seemed to call me and--" she paused. "There's something about Grace," she said painfully.

"Look inside, Karen," Davis said, holding the humidor.

"I can't."

Mignon lifted Karen's hand and patted it. "Grace has waited for fifteen years, child. She has waited, and now, she can rejoin her love. He is in the humidor."

A shudder ran through Karen as a trickle of blood dripped from her hand. "Another little one?" she questioned, staring down at the ornately carved wooden box.

Davis lifted the lid.

"He is beautiful," Mignon said, urging Karen to look inside.

"You said he's been dead fifteen years," Karen said, looking into the ornate box. "How can that be--he's so..."

"It is the process I learned from my family. Each generation, only one child is taught. It takes a long time because of the waxes. See how beautiful he is... just as I said."

Karen stared into the humidor, unable to believe her eyes. A man, slightly longer than Grace, lay with his hands folded across his chest, wearing a black tuxedo, with the tails positioned beside his legs. His face, though wrinkled, appears relaxed and peaceful. "He is dressed like a groom." The beginning of a smile creased Karen's face.

Only Mignon took note that Karen never described him as looking like a doll. *Karen has been sent to us, and just in time.* "She has been without him for so long. See, look closer, there is a space waiting for her. Now they will be together forever."

"But, why the humidor? Shouldn't we bury them with respect--in the normal manner?" Karen asked.

"It is the way it is supposed to be." Davis moved closer, invading Mignon's space.

"They are protected and preserved." He sighed, trying to keep his voice controlled, Davis continued. "Maybe the word *tradition* would mean something to you."

Karen turned, trying to focus on his meaning. "This has gone on long enough to be a *tradition*?"

"How could I expect you to understand," Davis said.

"Then, why don't you explain since I'm part of this now," Karen insisted.

"No. Go upstairs."

The master had given his order. Lisa grabbed Karen's arm to lead her away.

Mignon came up behind the two women and placed a gentle touch on Karen's back. "Please," Mignon said. Karen opened her clenched fist and lay Grace's little body into her hands. "I will take good care of her."

Karen offered a weak smile, feeling the touch of someone else. She shook off the offending hand and ran up the stairs, into the bath, and locked the door. She could hear the phone ringing and heard the answering machine come on. The voice sounded like Bob's, but she couldn't be certain. It didn't matter--not nearly as much as cleaning her hand.

How could one tiny little body make so much blood? She turned on the water, waited for it to warm, then stuck her hand under the faucet. *"Oh, dear God!"* she cried, nearly falling to her knees. The more she rinsed, the more the wound bled. *"This isn't good.* The water turned cold. She reached for towel after towel, fear consuming her, as each white towel turned crimson.

"I'm gonna bleed to death," she told her reflection in the mirror, and then it transformed. Grace's face stared back at her. "I didn't mean to hurt you," she whispered to Grace. "I only wanted to know." Grace slowly nodded, and her image faded.

Droplets of blood trailed behind Karen as she walked back to the bedroom. "This needs stitches," she said, squeezing the last clean towel tightly around her hand.

She opened the wardrobe. Out popped the familiar gown. Is everything in this room the same as it is in the little house downstairs? "Why does she have my things?" Karen never wondered if the question should be asked the other way around.

She pulled herself together, enough to slide her suitcase from under the bed and grabbed a pair of blue jeans, a tee shirt, and some socks. Clothes changed, she picked up her purse and keys. The wardrobe still stood open. She addressed the object as if it could help her. "Close, won't you?" She kicked at the door. It creaked back open. "Great! Now I've broken you, too." She pushed against the door. Again, it opened. "Fine! Stay open. I'm getting out of here." The floor board groaned as she stepped across it. "Stop that!" she demanded.

She moved down the staircase, listening and hoping against hope that Lisa had also been sent to bed. Voices shook her. Reaching the foot of the stairs, she crouched down behind a broad-backed chair.

"Did you lock her in?" Davis asked.

"Don't have to. The wardrobe will open when she gets to the bedroom door."

His eyebrow lifted as he glared at Lisa. "Why? Is it booby trapped?"

"No," she almost laughed. "It's just this old house. The board is unleveled and, when you step on it--along with the wardrobe being warped--it pops open."

"Well, it opens, so what?"

"It has a screeching creak like nails scratching a blackboard. You can hear it all over the house. If she's trying to leave, the wardrobe will be our alarm bell."

Karen replayed the event in her head. She'd closed the wardrobe door over and over again. It hadn't made a sound.

A growl came from deep in Davis' throat. "How bad do you think she cut herself?"

"I don't know."

He shrugged. "Maybe Mignon can tend to her," he said and walked out the front door.

Lisa pulled the heavy drape back from the window and watched him drive away. Karen's car was still in the driveway and the screeching sound had not come, so Karen had to be asleep. There was no need to bother her. Davis tended to be overly cautious. Lisa yawned. "A little more rest is what I need, too," she told herself. "Karen will need attention soon enough."

Still hidden behind the chair, Karen watched as Lisa climbed the stairs. Too frightened to wait any longer, she fled out the kitchen door. Her hand had begun to ache and it took all her strength to hold her keys. For the first time in her life, she was glad she owned a straight shift which would make for a quiet escape. She got in the car, stuck the key in the ignition, and stifled a gasp. She positioned her foot on the graveled drive and, using it as a lever, began to push the car backwards. It didn't move. "Crap," she whispered. "What now?" She dug her toe into the gravel and pushed harder.

"Why won't it move?" she whispered, then glanced down on the console. "Right, stupid..." she told herself, lowering the brake and shifting into neutral. It began to move, slowly, silently rolling backwards into the street. She turned the key in the ignition, shifted into first, and floored the gas peddle. Blood continued to seep through the towel she'd wrapped around her hand.

I should've paid more attention to this town. She felt she needed to head south, without knowing why. *North would be home, Stupid.* Shifting into third gear caused her hand to spurt blood. "I need a hospital," she muttered. The keen reporter's mind that she so longed for didn't seem to be working. *You sent me here, Bob. What do you know? What do I know? Grace... her name is Grace. Who told me that?* "Maybe I dreamed the whole thing," she said. "Maybe I've lost my mind."

The farther she drove, the more desolate the world became. To continue was fruitless. She squinted, trying to see a spot in the road to turn around. A narrow dirt alley appeared up ahead on her right. She slowed, then quickly turned into it, weaving through the dark, then stopped.

At the end of what she decided had to be a driveway, she saw a small house. The headlights lighted the old structure that looked as if it had fulfilled its duty as sentinel through the ages.

Curiosity got the better of Karen. She lifted her foot off the brake, slowly lifting the clutch as she shifted into neutral, and coasted up closer to the house.

A figure beckoned to her, as if she were expected. "I've driven to Mignon's." Again the old woman's wave of welcome coaxed her. Karen pulled the car to a stop and cautiously got out.

"This is your house?"

"Yes, yes, come in, child," Mignon said, taking the towel from around her bloodied hand. "It hurts?"

"It won't stop bleeding," Karen said, wincing as the air hit it.

"I will see to..."

"Mignon, you don't understand. I need to see a doctor," Karen said, biting her lip as Mignon lifted her hand.

"I am a nurse. Or, I was, a long time ago. I am a bit old for that now," she said, inspecting the wound. "Come, I will find something for it."

Karen followed Mignon to the back of the house and onto a small-screened porch. Rustic cabinets put together with hooks and wire held odd-shaped bottles and colorful bags. A large bowl with a toad in it sat on a mill bin. A well stood in the center of the porch with a rusted bucket pushed up against the turn wheel.

Mignon pulled drawers and lifted flaps that covered shelves, then approached Karen with a swab and a little brown bottle. When she opened the bottle a horrible odor filled the room.

"What is that?" Karen asked, covering her nose.

"A little sulfur powder. I will dab some on your hand, tape it shut, and you will be good as new."

"Sulfur powder?"

"Yes'm," Mignon said, dipping the swab into the bottle of yellow powder and stirring it up, then liberally sprinkling the substance onto the open gash. "Now, we will tape it closed. Mind you now, you musn't get it wet for a couple of days."

"It already feels better," Karen said in wonderment, thinking of how odd Mignon seemed. "I never heard of sulfur powder."

"It 'tis an old remedy." She winked and said, "and maybe a bit of magic."

"I don't believe in magic."

"You believe in Grace."

The mention of the tiny being brought tears to Karen's eyes. "Did you..."

"Yes," Mignon said. "She will join her love, just like she wanted."

"Was she really the last one?"

"No, of course not. Just like I'm not the last, nor are you."

"But, why did Lisa say--"

"Davis told Lisa that so she would take good care of Grace."

"What's with him anyway?"

Mignon shrugged. "He is as he is."

Karen glanced down at her hand. "I was sent here to do a

story. I was so excited. But, everything's gone so wrong."

Mignon stood silent. "What comes is meant to be, child."

Karen turned a quizzical eye toward Mignon. "My killing someone was *meant to be*?" Karen moved toward the door. "You know, don't you," Karen said. "You know things like that, even things I'm thinking and haven't asked yet." She took a deep breath. "Why do you keep talking about magic."

"You must believe in something," Mignon said softly. "Why are you here?"

"Because Bob thought I could write something for his magazine."

"Didn't you pray for a chance like this?"

Karen refused to look up, or answer, the old woman.

"Maybe magic is a prayer that you have forgotten, or a wish that you don't really believe will come true."

"Where have you put Grace?"

Mignon smiled. "Do you always change the subject when you don't want to face yourself?" Mignon busied herself with putting up the medicines and folding the bloody towel. "Wouldn't you rather see the other one?"

"*Other one?*"

"I told you she wasn't the last."

"How did these little people come to be?"

"When the time is right, you will know."

Karen wiped her nose. "I have so many questions," she said, as the thoughts spun around in her head.

"Yes, child. You do," Mignon said. "Sometimes you find the answers," she said, and smiled. "And, sometimes you must accept not ever knowing the answers."

"So much has happened since the meeting at the Inn," Karen said, absently massaging her hand. "I don't know why I ran out on Lisa. She'll be looking for me."

"Maybe," Mignon said, softly.

Karen swayed, unsteady on her feet. "I'm so very tired."

Mignon wrapped an arm around Karen's waist and led her

to a cozy room with a double bed, a nightstand, and a white rag rug spread at the foot of the bed. White plaster walls sparkled the multitude of flickering candlelights that filled the room. "Rest here a while, child," Mignon said.

Karen sat down on the bed, her mind holding on to thoughts of Lisa and Davis. *I don't trust them.* She passed out as the weight of everything forced her into a deep slumber.

Mignon smiled, blew out the candles, and tiptoed out of the room.

Chapter 4

Mignon stood admiring herself in the wall mirror. She loved her white robe which seemed to grace her mammoth figure. She smiled, attaching the long lacey train to the back of her pearl tiara, then placed it, as if a crown, on her head. She gracefully moved to the living room, lowered herself onto the sofa, and waited.

The sound of crunching gravel on the drive told her they'd arrived.

Davis got out of his car and slammed the door.

"Wait, Davis!" Lisa screamed, bolting out of her car.

Davis continued, rushing to the front door and, without knocking, shoved it open.

Lisa ran in, just a second behind him.

"Madame," Davis said, " Karen's car is outside."

Lisa stepped forward as if to speak. Davis silenced her with his pointed finger, then continued with Mignon. "I'm warning you, Mignon," he said.

"*You* are warning me?" Mignon almost sneered. "I think not." The soft but intense sound of her voice rolled across the walls and down around their feet like sea foam. Never had her authority loomed larger.

The sound of voices floated through the house awakening Karen. She sat up in the bed, wincing as she put weight on her wounded hand. She looked around the room, feeling safe, until she realized that there was no way out. No door. Only white unending walls in a room with no escape. She sat completely still trying to discern the voices.

"She will not be yours," Mignon said.

Davis fought to control his anger. "I've waited my whole life. It's my legacy! You must fulfill your mission."

"Karen will be kept safe--but, apart from you!"

His hands balled into fists. "What about Grace?"

"She's an example of how wrong the world can go," Mignon said. "Didn't you see her pain? Life without him took her spirit away."

His face went red. "You're denying me my life?"

Mignon shook her head. "I raised you, Davis. I gave you what you needed."

"You never told me the truth! Do you know how hard it was growing up here, with a black woman as a mama?"

"Everyone here knew I wasn't your mama."

"Fine, so what were you? My mentor? You knew my heritage, my destiny-- and you denied me it." The fury in his face grew. "I had to search the whole world to discover what is mine. And you knew it was right here in Dundury." He started pacing in front of her. "I know now, Mignon. I know why Sherman never destroyed Dundury." He shook his fist at her. "I know what he discovered here," he threatened through tightly-clenched teeth. He stopped pacing, then leaned into her face. "I know why he tried to burn the whole of Georgia," he whispered

Mignon grew more concerned with each whispered word. How could she keep Karen safe from him? A quick prayer escaped her lips; she looked at Lisa, then back at Davis.

"What did you promise this one," she said, jerking her head toward Lisa. It was a cruel thing to say, but Lisa had been a fool.

He turned to Lisa and snickered. "I told Lisa she was my choice. I tried with all those ladies. I went to the stupid parties, followed all the rules," he said, searing a look at Mignon. "But, then Karen was sent here." He didn't see the tears that ran down Lisa's face.

"You will die a horrible death if you fight the fates," Mignon said with the full authority of her station. "The choice has been made. You are *not* the one." Mignon sat back on the overstuffed couch; her decree had been issued.

"You're a crazy old witch-woman! You think you know so much." He paced in front of her like a panther poised with purpose, eyes blazing contempt.

"I'm the only one who knows the magic," Mignon said.

"Not anymore!" His look burned deep into her soul. "I found the magic."

"You've stored up the wrong treasures, Davis," she said.

"I'm ready now. You'll never win against me." A rush of cold invaded the room as he strutted passed her. The door slammed after him.

"Mignon?"

"Yes, Lisa."

"I guess I'm on your side now."

Mignon stood up, walked to her, and patted her hand. "You're not disappointed, then?"

"No, I guess I realized something when the clothes fit Karen. I think I'm actually relieved," she said, gently pulling her hand free of Mignon's and slowly walked out the door.

A broad smile flushed Mignon's face. All would be well, she knew it; but how she dreaded the journey to the end. Her reverie was broken by an insistent knocking. "I'm coming, Karen."

"Mignon, I can't get out." Panic filled her voice.

"Look at the walls, child."

"The walls are all white plaster!"

"Look closely. Do you see flowers?"

Karen ran her hands along every inch of wall space. Suddenly, a faint pattern leapt out at her. "Yes, I do. It's just one small panel of flowers pressed into the wall."

"Well?" Mignon asked with a giggle in her voice.

"That wasn't there before," Karen said.

"You didn't see before. You must learn to see all things."

"Okay, I see it. Now, what do I do?"

"Find the smallest flower and push it," Mignon said.

Karen pushed. A click sounded and the door popped open.

"Just like magic," Mignon said when Karen's face appeared.

"Magic, again," Karen said, wrinkling her nose.

"Did you rest, child?"

"Yes, until I heard a voice that sounded like Davis."

"Yes, he was quiet upset."

"Why?"

"Come with me, child. We must put Grace to rest," Mignon said, not wanting to discuss the confrontation.

"You'll bury them, then?"

"In a fashion. They are together in the humidor. Their time has come, child. It is proper."

Karen followed Mignon to the living room. "Why a humidor"

Mignon smiled. "It is part of the process I learned. It keeps the proper humidity." She continued, "It is what I was taught, and the way things must be."

"Are there really others?"

"Maybe in far away places," Mignon said turning and touching Karen's hand. "Come, I need you," she said.

"*My* help?" Karen asked.

"To pray and to sing. Come on," Mignon said, hurrying out the back toward the wooded area beyond her property.

"Hurry, child, we must get out back before dark. The woods start just past my garden." She hastened beyond a tree, and then, was out of sight.

"Mignon," Karen cried out, her voice shaking, "where are you?"

"Here child, just a few more steps."

An old tree stump stood in the center of the path, hollow and decaying, and seeping a strange and heavy odor.

"Do you know the Lord's Prayer?"

"Of course."

"Then, say it now," Mignon said.

Each stood still, softly praying the words in unison. After a moment, Mignon lifted her tiara and placed it on the ground. She pushed up her sleeves, and began digging at the dirt and dead leaves that had filled the stump. After placing the humidor snugly into the spot, she untied the tiny burlap bundle from around her neck, opened it, and poured the contents into the chasm.

"What is that?"

"Tobacco leaves first," she said, then dug at the mound of dirt, until the stump was filled."

Karen stood wondering about the significance of the tobacco leaves.

As if reading her mind, Mignon smiled. "Tobacco is an offering the Indians make, it purifies and keeps away evil." Karen nodded and took a reverent step backward as Mignon took her hand. "We will sing now." Her words were in a language Karen had never heard and yet, they evoked a calm and peace. Shooting stars drew their gaze to the heavens.

"I must go back to Dundury," Karen said.

Mignon nodded. "All will be well there," she said, and with hands joined, they silently walked the path back to the house.

"You've made me feel so much better, Mignon."

"You mustn't take your strength from me, child," Mignon

said, switching on a light, then suddenly recoiling as she glanced down on the small blue box below the lamp.

Karen moved closer.

"He's been here again," Mignon gasped.

Karen reached for the box. "It says Lucifer's?"

"He's left it for us."

"Who did?"

"Davis. He's angry."

"For heaven's sake, Mignon... it's an old match box."

"Yes... very old and... from the times he holds in such reverence," Mignon said. "The gown Lisa gave you, the historical society meetings, all honoring the War."

"But, what does this box have to do with the Civil War?"

"It's part of the horror...the fire, Karen. It's a sign," she said, slowly sitting down, and closed her eyes.

Karen pushed the little draw. "It's empty, it can't possibly harm us. As for a sign, well, I'm really getting tired of all the mumbo-jumbo mystery, Mignon. Why don't you tell me what's going on?"

Mignon suddenly looked very old. She opened her eyes; their gaze settling on Karen. "Did you ever wonder how Dundury survived, preserved intact, as if time stood still?

"Obviously, Sherman didn't burn it."

"Sherman left us be for a reason," Mignon said.

"But he tortured the rest of the South..." Karen said, sitting on the chair across from Mignon. "He refused to follow his orders."

Surprise covered Mignon's face. "You know of this?"

"I'm a Southerner, remember?"

"Yes, and taught to hate... as have so many," she sighed.

"The pain and the horror were passed down, Mignon. I've done the research. Sherman ignored General Order 100 which specifically directed that civilians were not be harmed. Sherman ignored that Order and waged war on innocents--the women and children, burning and killing everything and everybody who lay in his path--forever changing the way war would be fought." Karen paused, overtaken with the tears that filled Mignon's eyes and flooded her lush caramel skin.

"No, child, that is what the world knows. It is only here, in Dundury, where the truth lies.

"What truth, Mignon?"

"That poor man ravaged the whole of Georgia--because of what he found here..." *Twenty years before the war.* "Sherman let loose an evil so intense...so vile that it still lives among us."

"*Poor man!*" Shock overtook Karen.

"I carry the blood of many nations in my veins, a mix of all the colors of the world," Mignon said in a near whisper as her tears flowed. "I know things that have been passed down to but a very few."

This is madness, Karen thought. *I've been under the care of a crazy woman.* A searing pain shot through her hand, forcing her to uncontrollably rub the ripped skin; her eyes went wide with surprise. The gash had closed completely; the skin had metamorphosed into a scar of an indescribable color.

"There is a devouring evil here, child, an all-consuming wickedness that invades and corrupts a soul, until the soul is transformed."

"I don't understand."

"You cannot make the decision for yourself."

"What decision?"

A deluge of sadness filled the old woman. "Time is short, child. All will take place within the week."

Karen stood up. "What will take place in a week?" Mignon remained silent. Karen picked up her purse and keys. *What was it that Sherman found here in Dundury*, she thought as she turned and walked out of the house.

She kept the box of Lucifer's. Fire will come to that girl-- the kind that sears the heart, Mignon thought closing her eyes and clasping her hands.

Ava Lindsey Chambers

Dundury

Chapter 5

The dark was oppressive in a sinister kind of way, as though she were skirting the edges of evil. This night the stars merely blinked before retreating behind the clouds that drifted across the heavens, as tall pines blocked the intermittent glow from the moon.

"Well, if I can't see, no one can see me either," Karen said in an effort to comfort herself as she opened her car door and slid onto the car seat. Headlights popped a stream of white light from behind her. The sound of slow crunching footsteps on the gravel froze her body in place.

"I see you found the matches."

She recognized his voice. Karen looked down; they were still in her hand. "Did you leave these?"

"Maybe," Davis said.

"I think they scared Mignon half to death."

"But not you?"

"No, Davis." *They terrified me,* she admitted to herself, *but you'll never know it.* "You don't scare me." Her heartbeats throbbed in her hand.

"I came for you," he said, kneeling down beside the driver's window, and smiled.

"Forget it."

"You don't seem to understand, my dear."

Karen's fear gave way to anger. "I came here to do a story about the Inn. But, you know what, Davis, Dundury doesn't exist--not in books, and not on any map--and I want it to stay that way."

"I'm the one you were sent to interview."

"I don't care."

"Yes, you do," he said, leaning into the window. "How's your hand?"

She fought that same burning urge to massage her palm. "Move out of the way," she said, turning the key in the ignition and pressing down on the clutch.

"I was very pleased that you came. Don't you want your story?"

"Not any more."

"Come back to town... I'll give you the whole story. A true life account--one guaranteed to curl your hair."

"I have hot rollers," she said, flooring the gas, and fishtailing the car.

Thoughts of survival raced in her head as the squealing tires hit the pavement. *Lisa has my things. Maybe I should just drive back to Atlanta. My hand hurts...my head hurts.* The decision was made. "I need my things."

She glanced at the clock on the dashboard, it was eight-thirty. "Lisa, you'd better be there." Karen shifted gears and slowed the car to a crawl, moving through the deathly silence of Dundury. *Why do I feel so afraid?* she thought, pulling into Lisa's driveway. The house was in darkness, moonlight had cheated even the shadows.

Karen's nerve caught up with her, after three failed attempts to knock on the door.

Relief covered Lisa's face as she opened the door. "Hurry,

come in," Lisa said, pulling Karen inside and shutting the door behind her. "Did Mignon send you?"

"No, I need my things."

"Are you going to stay?"

Karen felt Lisa's fear. "Yes, I'll stay tonight and leave in the morning."

"No! No! You have to leave before Bob--"

"You heard from him?"

"Yes, but he mustn't come here. Do you understand? He must not come to Dundury."

"Why?"

"It's not safe for him--or you either."

"I'm so damned exhausted, Lisa. Let's sleep on it, okay?"

"*Sleep?*"

"Yes, Lisa," Karen said. "The thing that happens when you put your head on the pillow and close your eyes."

Karen walked toward the stairs, shuddering as she passed the little house still standing in the middle of the floor. *Is it evil that I feel?* She took the stairs, two at a time.

Lisa turned the dead bolts on the doors, followed Karen up the stairs, and once inside her room, she pushed a chair under the doorknob, climbed into bed--clothes and all--and stuck her head under the pillows. Muddled prayers were her mantra before sleep took possession.

Karen pulled on her pink pajamas and hauled herself up onto the bed, and then, the squeak pierced the silence. "What now?" The strange sounds of the house began to annoy her. "Who's there?" Karen called out.

"It's Bob. Get up! We've got to hurry!"

"Where are you?"

"In the armoire," he whispered.

She slid off the bed, careful not to thump the floor, and moved quietly to the wardrobe, tilting her head in confusion. "How did you get in there?"

"Doesn't matter," he said, reaching for her. "C'mon!"

"I suppose you're the lesser of all the evils in Dundury."

"Evil?" What has she discovered, Bob wondered.

"Yes, your buddy Davis has been stalking me--and he's definitely evil."

"Davis isn't evil, he's desperate and very ill."

"Ill, as in totally *crazy*?" she whispered, looking behind her to the bedroom door.

"Alright. Now c'mon."

"In there?"

"Yes. It's a passageway down to the cellar and outside."

"And then, where?"

"Back home."

"Let me put on my clothes."

"There's no time."

"I'm not going anywhere in my pajamas!"

"You can't stay here, Karen."

"Really? Well, *you* sent me here!"

The sound of a slamming door, followed by voices startled the both of them. Karen recognized one voice; it was Davis. The other she couldn't place.

"Oh, God! He's here," Bob whispered, watching as she shoved her legs into slacks and tugged on the zipper.

"Who is it," she asked, turning from him and jamming one arm, then the other, into her shirt.

"He was in my office the day you came--the one in the long dark coat. I know you saw him."

"Who is he?"

"Never mind." The expression on Bob's face touched her heart. She slid her feet into her shoes, just as he jerked her into the armoire.

The loud squeak of the door signaled their departure.

Lisa jumped out of bed, pulled the chair away from the door, and ran down the stairs. She slammed smack into the old man.

"She's gone," Lisa panted. She stepped back, away from

them and stared at the man. She recognized the coat. "Did you hear the armoire squeak?" The two men ignored her.

"Search the house," the old man commanded. "I know Bob is here. He came for her."

"No," she said. "Davis wants her."

The man turned and faced Davis. "Is Mignon helping you?"

"You don't understand, Kittendorf. I'm the one," Davis said. "You're too old to change the course of things. I now have the power."

Lisa's eyes widened at the name, "You're Kittendorf?" she stammered.

"I am," he said, grabbing her hand and dragging her out into the night.

"Where are we going?" Lisa asked, trying to pull free.

"To Mignon," Kittendorf grunted.

She fell before she could say another word.

"Get up!" Kittendorf ordered.

Davis followed after them. "Need some help, old man? Maybe we should team up together," he taunted Kittendorf as he helped Lisa to her feet.

Kittendorf snarled at Davis, then led the two deeper into the darkness.

"I can't see," Karen said, holding tight to Bob's shirt sleeve.

He pressed the button and his flashlight dropped a puddle of light on the narrow platform that was barely big enough for the two of them.

"It feels as if we're going into the bowels of the earth?"

"No, only about thirty-five steps." He lifted her hand, put it on his shoulder, and took one step downward. "Stay behind me and hold onto my belt." They finally made it to the bottom of the abyss.

"Where are we?"

"The cellar."

He steadied himself against the joist, trying to listen as dust sifted down from the floorboards and into his eyes.

"Bob?"

"What?"

"Could you shine the flashlight around a little?"

"Sure," he said, shining the light on the wall. He lifted the short curtain away from the narrow window at the top of the wall, wiped it with his shirt sleeve, then turned to Karen. "Better?" he said.

"Yeah," she said, walking through the musty subterranean level as the moon's light beamed down on them. "Look at all this stuff," she said, glancing at the trunks scattered about. Lamps stood like sentinels on top of crates, while odd chairs and tables, long left unused, sat cracked and rotting. Draped curtains covered shelves near the walls. Karen lifted the fabric. "What's this?"

Bob glanced in her direction. "Looks like canning jars of vegetables put up from the garden."

"Who did all this work?"

"Mignon, I guess," he said, listening again for Davis and Kittendorf. "Nobody else bothers much about canning anymore." His eyes settled on her again and guilt consumed him for having sent her to Dundury.

"Are they gone?"

"I think so," he said, feeling the warmth of her on his shoulder.

They moved slowly through the dimly lit basement, stepping over discarded chairs and squeezing between the stacks of trunks. Karen grabbed Bob's shoulder.

He turned around to face her.

"Look," she said, stepping up to a box filled with narrow drawers. "I've never seen anything like this." She opened one of the drawers. The smell of it's contents overpowered her.

"What is this," she asked, stifling a sneeze, as she leaned closer to the drawer. Another sneeze seized her.

"It's an old fashioned medicine chest. It was my great, great grandmother's." He smiled at the cute way she covered her nose.

"Hand me that light," she said, peering into the chest. Box after little box was perfectly aligned within each tiny drawer. "What is this?"

"Herbs."

"Did your grerat-great-grandmother live in this house?"

"For a while," he said, pacing the floor. "I've always just called her Grandmother--skipping the *greats*."

"Aren't we under Lisa's house?"

"Yes."

"So, are you two cousins or something?"

"No, her ancestors moved in after mine left."

"And, your family left during the war?"

"What war," he asked, continuing down the cellar path.

"The Civil War, dummy."

"No, my grandmother left before the war started. The story goes that one day she found a man in the woods who'd seen something that frightened him out of his mind. She brought him back to the house where he stayed in a stupor for several days. Then, one night he disappeared. Some say she went with him. Some say he told her what he'd seen and she went mad and disappeared into the night, too."

"That's weird," she said, following behind him. "So Lisa's family just moved into the grandest house in town?"

"Lisa's great-great-grandmother was my grandmother's cook. She had come in, started baking her bread, and fixing breakfast for the mistress that day. When she went upstairs, my great-great-grandmother was gone. As the good and loyal servant that she was, she continued to come everyday. Everyday turned into forever for Lisa's family."

"So, the house and everything in it is really yours?"

"Yes, but I don't want it. It's tainted."

"Because of the man who was brought here," she said, quickening her steps and trying to keep up with him. "So, who was the man?"

Bob stopped without warning and Karen plowed into his back knocking the wind out of him and the flashlight out of his hand.

"We're back in the dark, Bob."

"The damned thing could be anywhere," he said.

"Did you touch my foot?"

"No."

"Find the light, dammit."

"I'm trying," he said.

"Well, try harder!"

"I think I got it." A beam of light was her reward.

"Shine it this way--there's something down here with us."

"Did you see something?"

"Not in the dark." Karen suddenly squealed. "Something just touched me!"

Fear paralyzed Bob. "Let's get out of here," he said, aiming the light in her direction. "It's this way, I think," he said, before tripping on a crate.

"What happened... Did something grab you?"

"No, I tripped," he said, sitting down on the crate. "I'm trying to remember this place--I haven't been down here in years," he said, shining the light along the cavern wall.

"There's a torch on the wall," Karen said. "Right there." Her hand covered his. "To your left... right there!"

"How're we gonna light it?"

"The packs of Lucifer's back in that chest."

A knot tightened in his stomach. "How do you know about Lucifer's?"

"Davis left a pack at Mignon's."

His fingers cut into her shoulders. "Was the box empty or full?"

"Is this the pessimist, optimist question?" she asked, throwing off his hands as she waited for his answer.

"Karen," he said with authority.

"Empty. It was empty, Bob. I have it here in my pocket."

"That's it then, fire will purge. Just like Sherman."

She sighed and rolled her eyes. "Mignon and I talked about this Sherman thing. You know, people all over the world think it's laughable that the South refuses to let the war end."

"You're Southern, don't you love the romance?" he asked. "Isn't that worth preserving?"

"Well, sure. Hoop skirts and barbecues are good, but what about the slavery?" The war was about stopping evil."

He reached for her hand. "Do you *really* believe evil can be stopped?"

"Yes, I do.

"Or, has evil only found a new face?"

"What's that supposed to mean?"

"Never mind," he said, standing and brushing off his pants. "Stay here while I go back to the chest and see if any of the match boxes are full."

He lifted the torch out of the wall mount and handed it to her. "Sit on the crate and hold this. I'll be right back."

"Hold this, he says. Like it'll help." Karen bit on her lower lip. *Leaves me in total darkness and...* Something touched her shoulder. The word *pray* invaded her senses. "I don't pray," she shouted. "It never worked for me!"

"Karen!"

At the sound of her name, she stood and ran in the direction she thought Bob had gone. Something--or someone-- with unbelievable strength grabbed her. She screamed and then, a hand closed over her mouth.

"It's me. Calm down."

She felt the arms loosening their hold. Tiny kisses soothed her fear. "Bob?"

"Yes. It's okay," he said, pulling her into his arms.

She didn't resist; until her senses told her what was happening. "Turn me loose! You're kissing me, for God's sake!"

"I thought you were scared."

"Of course I'm scared. You left me alone in a dark hole."

"Well," he said, stepping back. "I guess you're over it."

She ran her hands up and down her arms, then stood up straight and attempted a glaring look. "Yes, well... are we, or aren't we getting out of here?"

He gestured with the flashlight pointed down on the dirt floor. "Pick up the torch. I found some matches. Now that we can see better, I think we need to take a few things with us. Did you bring a purse, a bag, something like that?"

"Of course, I had so much time to pack--after I got dressed," she said, sarcastically.

He frowned, lit the torch, and stuck it into the base of a broken lamp. "Look in those trunks," he said. "I'm gonna get some of the medi-- uh-- herbs, to take to Mignon."

She was happy to ignore him, then turned and yanked a musty piece of fabric from a pile of--whatever. The top trunk was small and locked, but the massive one on which it sat was ripe to pilfer. A faded piece of scented tissue paper hid a trove of women's clothes; each soft to the touch which confirmed the great care that had been given to preserve them. Did the gown she wore to the historical meeting come out of one of these trunks? Were these items left by Bob's ancestor?

"I need a sack," he said, coming up behind her.

"Damn! Will you stop sneaking up on me like that."

"I'm sorry. We have to get these to Mignon," he said, holding the box of bottles."

"Just take it like it is..."

"No, we need to keep these potions in total darkness."

She rummaged through the tissue and clothes and pulled out a black cloth sack. "Here, this should do."

"Good!" he said, carefully setting the bottles into the bag. "Alright, let's go," he whispered, carefully lifting the sack in a way that would cause the least amont of noise.

"*Good. Let's go,*" she mimicked, following him down the dark earthen level. "Who was the man your grandma took pity on?"

"Sherman," he said.

"*William Tecumseh Sherman?* That's ridiculous."

"No, it isn't because he was in Marietta in 1844--"

"So?"

"Sherman rode all over Northwest Georgia and Alabama and--" Bob stopped short and Karen plowed into him again. "Sherman came here, to Dundury," he said, pointing the flashlight into an opening along the wall.

"He met your great-great-grandmother, and then, she disappeared?"

"Yes."

Karen laughed. "She ran away with Yankee Sherman!"

"Just forget it, okay. We've got to get to Mignon. We'll climb up there," he said, starting up the set of decaying steps.

When he reached the top step, he jumped up for the latch on the slatted wood panel above his head. A small plug of wood popped out. "This should take us up to Mignon."

This can't be right. Mignon lived miles out of town; they hadn't walked nearly long enough. "This can't be Mignon's house, Bob," she said as he jumped and grabbed hold of the casing around the opening in the ceiling.

He grabbed hold of the sack of bottled potions and then reached down and pulled Karen up and into what looked like another tunnel. There was barely enough room for them to stand up.

"We're behind the chimney wall. It'll be a little close for a while, until we're sure no one is in the room."

She was slap up against him, his arms wrapped around her waist.

"I suppose you're gonna kiss me again?"

"Do you want me to?"

She didn't expect to have to give him permission. "Surely you can move back a little," she said, drawing in a quick breath. "And, by the way, this isn't Mignon's--"

Voices and the slow cadence of shuffling feet interrupted her.

"Well, well. Look who's come for the festivities."

"Yes, do sit down."

"Is that Davis?" Karen whispered in Bob's ear. His cheek brushed hers as he nodded.

"And, of course, you have a plan," the raspy voice asked.

"Of course," Davis answered.

"I won't let you succeed, Davis."

Kittendorf's voice sent chills up Bob's back as he waited for Davis' response. Silence prevailed. There wasn't a sound; not a voice spoke, nor a movement made.

"Are they still there?" Karen whispered in Bob's ear.

He closed his eyes, his heartbeats intensifying as the scent of her worked its magic. "I don't know."

"Well, can't you open a door or something," she said, her words carried on another warm breath.

"Only if you want them to know we're here."

"What if they're gone?"

"What if they're not," he countered.

"What if you've been heard?" The voice sounded on top of them, it's meaning unmistakable.

"Was... was that Davis?"

Bob nodded, tightening his hold around her waist.

Her lips brushed his cheek. "Open the door, Bob..."

Dundury

Chapter 6

The fingers of time refused to release their hold on the panel door. With difficulty, it finally gave in to Bob's persistence, and then, he stepped over the casing and into the room. He reached back into the darkened hole and clasped Karen's hand.

Her shoes crunched the dried paint chips as she stepped from behind the wall; a pelt of cold air hit her face and she looked up to the high domed ceiling where ornate dentil molding framed a frescoe of angels smiling down on her.

Bob eased Karen closer to him.

"Good evening," Kittendorf said to Karen. A dense crop of thick gray hair framed a wrinkled face that resembled an apple doll. The dark coat that covered his frame exaggerated the size of him. "Can you speak?"

My God! The old man looks ancient, she thought as Bob came around her.

"Of course she can, Father," Bob said, stepping in front of her and blocking his father's penetrating stare.

"So, my son finally acknowledges me."

"Why are you here, Father?"

"Because you are. Don't you remember?"

"It's too late for that," Davis interjected. "I assume you've collected all the necessary ingredients, Bob."

"I have nothing--as you can see," Bob said, holding out his hands.

Davis pushed past them and stepped inside the hidden room; the black sack lay just inside its wall. "Ah... I knew you wouldn't fail me, Bob."

A look of futility covered Bob's face.

His father smiled. "Thank you, Davis. That should be easy to destroy."

"No!" Bob screamed, rushing at Davis.

"I told you this thing would not happen again," Kittendorf roared, advancing on Bob and colliding like two raging beasts whose onslaught knocked Karen to the floor.

Davis laughed. "Do not doubt its happening, old man," he said.

"Stop!" Karen screamed, trying to pull Bob and his father apart.

Davis grabbed her, holding tight to the sack. "You have done magnificently, Bob. I now have *everything* I need," Davis said through a sinister smirk, his lust-filled eyes settling on Karen.

Anger consumed Karen. "You sent me to this maniac... why?"

"No... no, Karen. I--"

Kittendorf lunged at Davis, but a deafening boom thundered the room as billowing smoke blinded them.

Karen rubbed her burning eyes. "Bob, I can't see you! Bob!" she screamed in the uncontrolled sensation of falling as darkness snuffed out her senses.

When she awoke, she found herself tied, gagged, and

bouncing in the back of a horse-drawn wagon, no it was a buckboard. The black sack she and Bob had filled lay beside her. She struggled, carefully anchoring her foot beside it, as she moved closer to the open end of the wagon. A deep rut in the road provided the bounce she needed; the sack tumbled off. That done, she worked to remove the rope from around her wrists.

"Davis! Stop this wagon and untie me!"

"Oh, so you're with me now. Lovely day, isn't it, my dear?"

"What?"

"It's such a lovely day for a country ride, don't you think?"

She rolled to her side, struggling to get to her knees. "Where's Bob and his father?"

"Back at the Inn."

Bob said we were going to Mignon's... "Where are you taking me?"

"To my home."

"I thought you lived at the Inn," she said, wiggling and fighting the tension of the rope around her wrists. "Stop this buggy and untie me!"

"No, darlin' I cannot do that," he said, smiling. "Besides, the Inn was consumed in flames when we left."

Flames--

"You'll love our home. We'll be taken care of for eternity, my darlin'," he said, glaring into her eyes.

"*We?*" she asked.

"Yes, ours will be a great and binding love."

In your dreams, you maniac! She fought the pain of the coarse rope cutting into her skin.

"Mignon will help us. We'll have our little house filled with little people, too," Davis said.

"Like Grace?"

He smiled the pleasure of his fantasies. "Mignon will see

to it."

"Are you telling me that Mignon made Grace?"

"Oh, I'm sure of it."

"How?"

"Well, now that is the secret. It goes back to the beginnings of time, I believe. Have you ever heard of Tom Thumb?"

"Yes, I know the story," ...*You moron!*

"You know then that the kindly Merlin talked to the fairy queen and, together he was born of a mother's love."

"I hadn't heard..." she said, twisting her wrists.

"It started that way in England, all those centuries ago."

There was no doubt in Karen's mind that Davis was mad. Fairy tales and sorcerers were children's stories which he, obviously, still believed. *And, what does that have to do with Mignon?* "Why do you want these little people, Davis?"

"Immortality, my love-- and the power they grant," he snickered.

"They can't be immortal, Davis. There'd be so many more around us."

"Are you so sure there aren't? Did you hear them in Lisa's house? Did you feel them touching you, my dearest?"

Karen only felt the fear bubbling in her belly. "Bob said you're sick?"

"Yes. I've tried all the great physicians' remedies, but still I grow weak."

"I've heard about cures coming out of the rain forest-- things doctors never imagined," she said.

He turned on the buckboard seat and smiled so lovingly at her. "How kind you are to think of helping me. I knew you would, my love."

"Exactly what is your illness?" *Besides the insanity!*

"It's an odd condition...one that is passed down through the Hamilton bloodline. I have a tendency to break out in boils which gets worse with each eruption. At some point, well, I don't know..." He shrugged.

Karen felt the rope giving way.

"The sickness was the catalyst for me," he said, turning and startling her. "I began to travel and to study all the things I'd never had time for. That's how I came upon the truth of our little people. Bob confided in me that his grandmother hadn't really disappeared, merely moved to a different realm."

Karen rolled her eyes, then judged the distance she would have to jump to be free of Davis. "What would make you believe a story like that?"

"I grew up in Dundury, my dear. I know its history."

The buggy bounced through another deep rut, almost throwing her over the side wall of the wagon. Davis grabbed for her, slowing the horse and turned around Panic consumed him. "Where's the bag?"

She felt the wet run of perspiration rolling down her back. "What bag?"

"You know very well what bag!" he screamed, his eyes frantically searching the back of the wagon. "What did you do with it?"

Davis abruptly pulled rein on the horse, turning and, curiously, appearing to be completely calm. He reached for her and pulled her onto the seat beside him, then tenderly looked into her eyes. "You and I will be so happy, my love." He leaned closer to her, brushing invisible dust from her shoulders, and then, he kissed her.

Karen recoiled; an involuntary action that she was helpless to control.

Davis looked up to the morning sky. "You will be my queen." The blue of heaven burst forth as if nothing were amiss on earth. "Of course, we won't be able to take rides like this into the countryside."

"But, it's so lovely and so romantic, Davis. Why won't we be able to take rides like this?"

Davis smiled and stroked her check. "Because Mignon is

being stubborn, refusing to allow me to build the carriage house where I want." *She's too confused to really understand what I'm saying*, he thought.

"So, build it somewhere else."

The most tender smile appeared on his face. "I knew you would come around, my love. Maybe I could--" he paused in contemplation.

If he thinks I'm on his side, maybe... "How will the little ones make us immortal?"

"They're part of another world, a powerful place."

That's not an answer. "How do we find them?"

"We must release them."

"How?"

His fingers dug into her cheek. "We must find that sack of potions. I need those powders."

"Then, we'll stay at your house--" she swallowed hard, "Together, forever?" Karen fought the urge to rip her hands free and jump from the wagon.

"Yes, darlin'. It will be more wonderful than you can imagine." He placed another gentle kiss on her lips. "I'll take you home, and then go and search for the bag. It was very naughty of you to toss it out."

"I didn't see the sack, Davis. It must have bounced off the back of the wagon."

A sudden slap across her face stunned her. "Don't ever lie to me," he screamed into her face. "I'll always know when you're lying to me." He cracked the reins across the horse's back. Karen slumped onto his shoulder.

After only a short ride, he pulled the wagon to a stop in front of a huge Georgian colonial. Lights illumined the front verandah and a black man of indeterminate age welcomed him. No words were spoken, just several nods between them as Davis and the old black man helped Karen down from the wagon. Davis didn't see that her hands broke free of the rope.

She tossed the rope to the old black man, stamping her

feet to force the blood back into her numbed legs, then followed Davis up the flight of stairs and into the mansion.

A glistening crystal chandelier hung above her; its countless tiny bulbs diffusing a soft light. Davis grabbed her arm, yanking her toward the red-carpeted staircase. Fear filled her as she caught sight of a tiny replica of the house sitting in the center of the main parlor floor.

"It's been ready for months," Davis said, pointing to the replica. "I'm certain some little ones will appear soon."

"Why does everyone insist on putting it in the middle of the floor?"

"We began the custom when Sherman came through. When he saw, well... " Davis shrugged. "Come see the rest of your new home, my dear," he said, pulling her up the winding staircase.

She followed, then tugged her arm, staring at the condition of what she first thought was wallpaper. Upon a closer scrutiny, it hardly seemed to be wallpaper at all. She frowned, following the long lines of red and blue streaks across the paper that had no determinant motif, or design. Tacks had been stuck into what appeared to be a focal point and, at the bottom of one corner was a kind of legend that hardly made sense to her.

"Do you like it, darlin'?" Davis asked, pointing to the faint lines. "It's a map of Georgia--1864." Excitedly, he reached for her waist and pulled her into his arms. "Sherman's infamous *march to the sea*," he said, nuzzling her ear. "Sherman and his men split their route... see, just north of Dundury. It's clear he deliberately planned that Dundury not be touched."

"*Deliberately planned?*" she asked incredulously.

"Of course," he answered. "I told you, Sherman respected our little ones." He turned her in his arms.

"Sherman *knew* about the little people?"

"He witnessed some of Dundury's greatest and most

historic moments." Davis' smile grew broader which told Karen there was much more to learn. "Look here, Griffin, Macon, and Milledgeville; the Yellow River--all the burning and looting before he even got to Atlanta. It's all marked."

Disgust filled Karen as she watched his gloating face. "He destroyed most of the state!"

"Yes, that was unfortunate."

"*Unfortunate?* He decimated an entire population... ruined our land, and destroyed our way of life. And you're telling me, Sherman and his troops just marched around Dundury because the monster saw some doll houses?"

He tightened his hold around her waist. "Because of the little ones, my dear." His voice remained calm in a whisper, as if explaining to a child. "Dundury enjoys a kind of wedded *protection*--one Sherman knew well enough not to disturb."

"Davis, I--"

"Come, this way--" he said, pulling her to the top landing. "I have topographical maps, battle maps, old maps with cities that don't exist anymore," he said.

Bob said Sherman was here before the war and that something in Dundury had scared him. The little houses and little people must have been here before Sherman came here? Karen's head began to ache again. "Davis, did other people in other towns know about the little people?"

"Yes, some did," he said, continuing down the hall. "There are clues everywhere. For centuries mankind has ignored the secrets that have been passed down to Dundury. We must all fight to save them," he said, walking her into a bedroom.

"But, Bob's father doesn't want to save it," she said.

"No, he thinks it's all evil. But, that's because of Grace," Davis said. "Evil, evil, evil."

"Why?"

Davis sunk down onto a plush velvet Victorian chair, perched like an old spinster about to share the juiciest gossip.

"Grace was Bob's grandmother," he said, leaning forward, then winked. "Philip, however, was *not* Bob's grandfather."

"So, what you're saying is that Grace had an affair?" Karen asked.

"Not any affair, an affair with her sister's husband. She waited for him all those years, because she needed Philip." Davis sat back and waited for Karen to absorb the full intent of his words.

That doesn't make any sense at all, Karen thought, slowly walking around the room.

The chair seemed to swallow Davis and, for a moment, she thought he was about to doze off. One step, then two, she moved closer to the door, then opened it.

An imposing man stood in the doorway; retreat was impossible.

"He's *my protector,*" Davis said through a confident smile, that worked its way into a yawn. "You'll be safe here while I go find the sack. Try to rest. Someone will bring you food and make you comfortable."

The burly giant walked her backwards into the room and pulled the door closed; the lock's clack a confirmation that there would be no escape.

Lush ivy intertwined the wrought iron that covered the windows--as effectively as bars. Karen gave into despair, though it was never something she was comfortable with doing. A plate of fruit on a table across the room beckoned her. Tears of frustration and disappointment flooded her eyes through uncontrollable sobs.

Davis strutted down the staircase in a princely fashion, walked through the massive double doors, and out into the night.

Mignon held all the secrets of life. She could increase a lifespan by a tenfold; it was well within her powers and yet, she vehemently refused--on more than one occasion. It had enraged him and forever altered the respect he once held for her. "You'll not refuse me this time, my dear Mignon," he said, heading toward the wood line.

His walk in the cool of the night brought him to Mignon's door in record time. He reached for the knocker and hesitated; voices echoed from within. Like a phantom, he moved to the window. *How did you find the courage to venture out into the night, Lisa--You twit!*

A slow grin took possession of his snarled lips. He reached into his pocket, pushed the tiny draw, and emptied out the match sticks. "That will do nicely," Davis whispered, placing the empty box of Lucifer's on the threshold. And night reclaimed the devil.

The cacophony of screaming owls and rustling trees confused Davis. He knew the land from the time of Sherman's invasion to the present. Every turn in the road, each hill, and every battle was suffused in his heart, as well as his mind. The years when drought parched the land, or those years when rainfall flooded the fields; he could spout off the dates as if they were a grocery list. Yet now, the task of walking back the way he had come proved impossible.

Over and over he found himself face to face with the same oak stump and, each time the fates positioned him in the same place, frustration overwhelmed him.

He kicked the old dead thing, slapped and spat, but the stump only grew stronger, resisting him and holding firm.

Sweat covered his body, starting at his forehead and running into his eyes while fiery blasts of pain shot up his arms. His legs gave way and with a final scream into the dead of the night, he collapsed.

"Mignon, did you hear something?" Lisa's face turned ashen as she held her breath, listening.

"Open the door," Mignon said.

"No, we mustn't," Lisa whispered.

"It is an unholy night. Open the door," Mignon said in a desperate whisper. Lisa hurried to comply, rushing outside and crushing the pocket-size matchbox under her feet.

"It's nothing, Mignon."

"Then come, child. We must hurry and finish our task." Mignon paused a moment then went to the door, making a point of sliding the dead bolt into place.

Lisa meticulously wrapped the ancient glass bottles and placed them between sacks made of animal skins. "Is that all?"

"No," Mignon said. "There's one more thing to be done." A tear fell from her eye as she made room for her pearl tiara. Withered fingers stroked the netting as if saying good-bye.

"Why are you sending this? I thought it was to be buried with Grace."

"It was, child. I took it back."

"Why?"

Searching her heart and struggling to speak, Mignon stifled a sob. "It will be my gift. It is all I have. Now, wrap it up, child. I'll give you the address."

Lisa followed her instructions, wrote the address on the front of the package, and promised to mail it on the morrow.

"Now go, child," Mignon said in a soft satisfied voice, then settled down to pray.

Lisa unbolted the door. She heard Mignon's pleading prayer and bowed her own head. "Help me do my part, Lord," she whispered, shifting the box under her arm and walked out to her car.

Ava Lindsey Chambers

Chapter 7

Karen struggled to stay awake in the strangeness of the house that Davis had said they would share. She tossed and turned, slid off the bed, even stared out into the darkness before returning to the four-postered bed. It was no use; sleep had won out.

Opening her eyes to the sun's bright rays brought a sense of relief. She stretched and yawned, and then a knock sounded at the door.

"Madame, your breakfast is served," the voice said before the door swung open. A plump, round-faced woman stood behind a serving cart. Her blue eyes seemed to dance in delight as her unpainted lips broke an infectious smile. "I hope this meets with your approval," she said, lifting the silver dome that covered a plate filled with soft-scrambled eggs, a mound of thick bacon slices, a stack of toast, and a deep dish of grits swimming in butter. A chilled silver pitcher glistened beside a crystal vase that held a single red rose.

"Thank you," Karen said, her hunger overpowering all other thoughts. "It looks wonderful!"

"Well, I hope you enjoy it," the woman said, fluffing the pillows behind Karen, then lifted the tray from the cart and positioned it over Karen's legs. She turned back to the cart and the basket of biscuits and the jar of preserves. "I didn't know if I should bring you sweet milk gravy or Mignon's figs," she said, her tiny white fingers pinching the top of Karen's hand. "I thought a little sweetness would be best," she said, turning to the tray and lifting the small plate of biscuits and jam.

"Did Mignon made these preserves?"

"Yes." The chubby woman giggled.

"Is she all right?"

"I suppose so," the woman said.

"Did Davis go to see her last night?"

"Oh, I wouldn't know about the master's comings and goings."

Karen lifted the fork. "I expected to see him."

"Yes...well, like I said, we never know about him."

"You serve him like a--"

"A *slave*," the woman said.

"He's obsessed with the Civil War," Karen said, dusting the biscuit flakes from her mouth.

"More obsessed with Sherman, if the truth be known," the pudgy little woman said, handing Karen another napkin. "Thinks he can discover why Sherman never burned Dundury."

"But, he did..." Karen said, swallowing the dried biscuit. "Find out, I mean."

"Did he tell you about things in Dundury? Is that why you came?" An intensely puzzled look covered the woman's face.

"No, I came to do a story about the Inn," she said. "My friend, or someone I thought was my friend, has a magazine...I was going to help him with an article about the old place."

The woman smiled through a patronizing grin.

"I really had no idea that things were so strange down here," Karen said, then leaned toward the woman and whispered, "But my editor, the owner of the magazine, well, he surely knew about Dundury. And, I'm furious with him."

"What's his name?"

"Bob Kittendorf."

The color dissolved from the woman's face. "How old is he?"

"Not much older than I am."

"Have you met his father?"

"Yes...it didn't go well," Karen said, shaking her head. "You know them?"

"I know *of* them," the woman said. "I'll leave you to finish your breakfast; I'll be back for the tray in a little while."

"Where are you going?" Karen asked as the woman opened the door. "I don't know your name."

"Ruth. I'm going outside, to hang some clothes on the line."

"I used to watch my mother hang clothes. May I help you, Ruth. I'll go crazy cooped up in this room."

"The master will be quite upset if he finds his lady hanging clothes," Ruth said with a wink.

"I wouldn't be his lady if I couldn't smooth things over a bit, now would I, Ruth?"

"I suppose," the woman said, considering Karen's confidence in the matter. She liked this girl. She had vowed, like those in her family before her, that she'd take care of Davis. This time, she hoped it would work out for the best. "I was instructed to make you feel at home," she said through a broad smile, her laughter tinkling like wind chimes through the room. "I'll come back and get you in a bit. Eat your breakfast," she said, then closed the door.

Karen placed the tray on the bed beside her and carefully

eased her legs over the side of the bed. *Where's the shower?* she thought, wondering what she'd do for a change of clothes.

Ruth reappeared. "You'll be wanting a shower," she said. "The master's room is down the hall. I'll bring you some fresh clothes."

"It won't be a ball gown, I hope."

"You are silly. My granddaughter is about your size. Well," she paused, studying Karen's height and frame. "She's a little heavier and not as tall, but I believe her things will do. I'll be back."

This house must be a lot newer than Lisa's if it has a shower. She pushed open the bedroom door and looked down the hall. Light filtered through soft sheer curtains on the three windows that were part of the hall, along with three vases filled with bright red roses, so red they almost appeared black; each taking center stage atop the marble tables that stood between each window. The house was comfortable and beautifully decorated, obviously, with a woman's touch. *I wonder if Ruth is responsible for the décor.*

The door at the end of the hall opened to the master's bedroom. In sharp contrast to the rest of the house, it was definitely a man's domain. Old books lined one wall, muddy shoes littered the front of the fireplace, maps lay curled on a table, and cigars overflowed ashtrays near the mahogany four-poster bed.

She turned, facing a beautiful life-size portrait of a woman whose eyes followed Karen as she roamed through the room. She stopped at a collection of paper weights, each filled with a different color that changed, *no, it's moving.* She reached to pick one up when Ruth suddenly reappeared. Karen jumped.

"You scared me half to death."

"I must get on with my chores. Here," Ruth said, handing Karen the clothes. "Go on through to the master's bath." She gave Karen a push. "Hurry, girl! It's not like I have all day."

"That picture..." Karen said, looking up to the portrait.

"It's Grace, isn't it?" She waited for a reaction.

Ruth nodded.

"Why is it here? I thought Grace was Bob's great-great-grandmother?" A sudden dawning came over her. "She is Bob's grandmother--isn't she?"

"I'll tell it all to you downstairs, at the line. Just hurry."

Would Ruth finally explain the whole story to her? The hot and cold knobs squeaked as the water gushed from the shower head. Despite the warm spray, a cold chill ran over her. She jumped out of the shower, soap still clinging to her, and pulled on the oversized clothes. With no sign of the fierce protector who had guarded her last night, she ran down the steps and out the front door.

The morning breeze danced through Karen's hair and kissed her cheeks. She followed the sound of singing around to the backyard. A wide ascending set of steps, apparently leading nowhere, barred her path.

"Ruth?"

"Yes, just come around the steps."

Karen stopped a moment to roll up the leg of her pants. "What are the steps--a highway to heaven?"

Ruth laughed. "They're mounting steps. The ladies climbed up in their riding habits so they could mount their horses."

"Makes sense, I suppose. Did Davis build them?"

"No, they were part of the original house." She pointed past some purple flowers twisting around the last few mounds of discarded bricks which had been part of the old foundation. "The lilac, which only grows around old houses, and these steps are all that's left of another time."

"Is this new house modeled after what used to stand here?"

"No, what stood before was..." Ruth paused to pickup the pillowcase she dropped. "The new house is traditional which suits Davis' imagination. It will be perfect, once it's finished."

"I suppose," Karen said, humming as she picked up a towel from the basket. "I guess you'll be glad when all the building equipment is moved," she said, the clothes pin her pointer as she punched the air toward the area beyond the clothes line.

Ruth pinched the pillowcase onto the line, then another, connecting them as a colorful rainbow across the narrow rope.

"I love hanging out clothes. It reminds me of my grandmother's house," Karen said. "They smell so good, too. Bet you hate when it's winter and you have to use the dryer."

"We have no dryer."

"Really?"

"This is the only way I've ever known."

Karen eyed Ruth. She was a pleasant looking, older woman. *But, not really so old,* she thought. "How old is Davis?"

"Oh, he's quite a young man," Ruth said.

Compared to what, Karen thought. "Then, he'll live to a ripe old age," she muttered under her breath. *With me as his prisoner.*

"He isn't well," Ruth said sadly.

"He thinks I can make him better," Karen said.

"Love makes all things better."

"He has some kind of plan for me, as if I have some special purpose."

"He has dreams, I suspect."

"*Dreams?*" Karen snickered; baiting Ruth didn't work. "He thinks he can live forever and I seem to be his means to that end."

"No, Karen. It's not possible."

"How can you be so sure?" Karen asked.

"Because Kittendorf won't let it happen," Ruth said, sliding her basket along the grass as she pinned the pieces that filled the line.

"But Davis did something to him."

Ruth's smile vanished. "What do you mean?"

"We were all together...there was a shot, I think... I'm not sure...the next thing I remembered was waking up in the wagon with Davis." She shook her head as if dislodging cobwebs that clogged her mind.

"Help me finish with the clothes. Then we'll talk." When they had finished, the two women walked to the steps and sat down.

"What can you tell me, Ruth?"

The woman lifted Karen's hands and patted them. "You must believe that Davis does not want to die. What you must understand is that he really wants the power and prestige that has been lost to his family."

"Was little Grace part of his family? And, who was Philip?"

"No. Grace, as you said, was Bob's grandmother. Philip was Davis' grandfather." Ruth paused, not sure of how much she should tell Karen. "Bob's father has seen things... horrifying things, it's why he's such a tenacious protector who vowed never to let evil escape again. The little ones are a sign..." she said, without looking up at Karen, her face reflecting a terrible sadness.

"But, Grace is gone," Karen said, squeezing Ruth's hand. "So, what is Kittendorf trying to stop?"

Ruth sat silent, then slowly looked into Karen's eyes. "Each time evil is unleashed, it becomes harder and harder to overcome."

"This has happened before?"

"Yes. Before the war between brothers."

"You mean, the Civil War?"

"Yes."

She's got to be kidding! "What did Kittendorf witness," Karen dared to ask.

"Grace was such a beautiful young woman--healthy, and so heavenly vibrant. Philip offered something that she thought she needed, and which she, unfortunately, longed for."

"I don't understand what you mean. How were they connected?"

Ruth's eyes looked out into the day and back into the past. "Kittendorf, Bob's father, had long known about Dundury and had brought his new bride here to continue the legacy. He had such dreams for their eternity together in a safe world, a secure life. Kittendorf had dreamed of a promised tomorrow that never dawned--because Philip had destroyed those dreams.

"When did Bob's father bring his bride to Dundury?"

"Before the war. We all came together."

"What war?"

"The war!"

"The Civil War?"

Ruth nodded.

Karen rolled her eyes. *You stupid old woman, you're as addled as the mad hatter.*

Ruth appeared to be in a trance. "Anger and hate seeped out. Mignon was there that day, with another little girl. They were learning from their grandmother; it was to be their final instruction."

Karen tried to visualize the two little girls, and the two men vying for the beautiful Grace, and a grandmother divining potions. *All this before the war--that would make Bob's father over a hundred years old!* "This sounds a little bizarre, Ruth."

"'Tis not," Ruth said defiantly. "You held Grace. You fulfilled the promise. When a little one dies, power is gifted. That's why Davis wants you. Power and status were lost to Davis and his family. He wants it back."

"So, you and all of Bob's family are pushing two hundred years in age? You're immortal, I suppose."

"No one lives forever, not humans, nor other creatures. It's the love that lasts. Don't you see, love never dies." Tears ran down Ruth's face and she made no attempt to wipe them away.

"Did Grace and Philip love each other?"

Ruth choked, turning and glaring at Karen. "Philip wanted Grace to tell him the secrets of Dundury. They met over there," she said, pointing to the burned out spot. "It was early morning and pouring down rain--*Tears from the angels*, Mignon always called them..." She paused, as if saying she couldn't continue.

"What happened?" Karen urged.

She hesitated. "Kittendorf was filled with rage. He thought Grace and Philip were--"

"Lovers?"

"It wasn't true. His thoughts were the madness of having been deceived--it was part of the evil that to this day winds through the world. Dundury is-- I've got more work to do." She abruptly stood up.

"Wait!"

Ruth shook her head, choked in the emotion that overwhelmed her. "I've got work to do!" She ran toward the front of the house and disappeared.

Will I ever learn the truth, she thought as something suddenly grabbed her shoulders and pushed her to the ground.

Ava Lindsey Chambers

Chapter 8

"Damn!"

"Be quiet," the voice whispered as a hand clamped Karen's mouth shut.

She yanked the offending hand away and spun around to her transgressor. "Bob! What are you doing here?"

"I came for you. You need my help and I need yours."

Karen shuddered through the chill of practicality that she likened to a splash of cold water that did wonders for the senses.

"We've got to stop the madness before someone gets hurt," Bob said as they stood nose to nose, staring into each others eyes. "I thought I'd lost you." His words came quite suprisingly.

"Where's your father...is he alright?"

"He escaped, again." Bob said, shaking his head. "I'm not sure where he is, much less *how* he is."

"I thought I heard a shot--was he hurt? I don't know how I ended up with Davis."

Bob stroked her cheek. "It was a blank. Father is the one who fired it. Davis was trying to save you."

"No, I don't think so," she said, shaking her head in variance with his words. "Davis has said some very bizarre things--he's made a quantum leap from being *ill*, to certifiably insane!"

"Davis had a hard time growing up, partly because the people of Dundury never accepted him."

"Because he's nuts!"

"That's not fair, Karen, he and I were best friends for the first ten years of our lives. Our families were--" he paused, "--connected."

"Yes, I know all that--your beautiful grandmother and his dashing grandfather."

Anger took possession as he squeezed his hands into fists, then jammed them into his pockets and took a deep breath. "My grandmother loved the arts, poetry, and music. My father's world, on the other hand, was steeped in magic--"

"Whoa! Wait a minute!" she said through the intensity of disbelief that fired her eyes. "You're telling me that your father--the *same* Kittendorf I saw yesterday--has lived since before the Civil War?"

Bob slowly nodded. "My family has been gifted with an extremely long lifespan because we have a duty to the world. I'm not sure how it started. I just know that's the way it is."

"And Davis?"

"We're cousins. But, his side of the family took a wrong turn."

"And, it started with Sherman?"

"Davis says so. The glory of the South was a world and a way of life in which my grandmother and father believed."

"Yes, and the whole world has loved the story of the old South," Karen said. "But, Bob, it's all been romanticized--"

"All I'm saying, Karen, is that those times were the precursor to the war and the intimate disease of unrestrained pleasure. All the beauty and glory carefully hid the truth."

"Which was?"

Bob walked Karen to the barren spot where the poplar tree once stood. "Sherman stumbled onto Dundury some time during his 1844 stay in Marietta. The story goes that he learned about the little people and, somehow, had witnessed the evil that the little ones suppressed from the world. He was a man in search of a life that, up until 1844, had been a life of chance. He'd been a soldier trained for battle--and glory. When he came to Dundury, his destiny changed. His desire was so great that nothing could have held back the evil. It filled him, drove him, and ate him alive.

"Is that what's happening to Davis?"

Bob nodded. "Davis' grandfather wanted power, too. Philip did, after all, pit two sisters against each other."

"And?"

"It was Philip who had unlocked the gateway to hell."

Karen rolled her eyes. "This is too much."

"Dundury *is* the gateway to hell--a place that must be forgotten."

Why? she asked herself in the horrible ache of needing to know.

"I don't know if I can prevent it from happening again."

"Another Civil War?"

Bob was deadly serious. "No, something much worse," Bob said, rubbing his sweaty brow. "The little ones fight a battle the world knows nothing about. It was preordained that my family would help them and save them. We are their protectors."

"Because little people aren't supposed to die..."

He couldn't find the words that would relieve Karen's guilt. He watched her fight the tears then brought her into his arms where she willingly took comfort in his unspoken love for her.

"Things happen, Karen."

"That's what Ruth was trying to tell me."

Ruth? How much did she tell you?

"I think she's supposed to care for Davis and his little people," she paused and took a quick breath. "And me."

"That's over now."

"No, Bob," she said, lifting her head off his shoulder. "Ruth is part of it, too. She knows too much about the Kittendorf's."

"I'd hate for my Father to know that someone else is giving away the secrets of Dundury. There is always a dark side lurking, Karen. We must be ever aware."

She stared at Bob then stepped back and away from him. "What about Mignon? What's her part in all this?"

"Mignon looked after Davis when he was very young," Bob said.

"As Bertha did for you?"

"Sort of." He hesitated.

"And?" she asked.

"Mignon holds the magic--the ingredients for the potions. She keeps the physical body well."

"She's not going to help Davis."

"No, I don't think that's what this is about. Father is involved with something much darker."

"Something that you agree with?"

"Part of me does."

"What about the part that doesn't?" Karen asked.

Bob let out a long and heavy sigh and looked up at the heavens. "I think Davis is going to die."

"Why?"

Tears filled his eyes. "Davis left Dundury and embarked on a world journey searching for a remedy because Mignon couldn't--or wouldn't--cure him.

"Do you know what will save him?"

Heat moved between them. He dared not kiss her again, but he couldn't keep from wrapping his arms around her waist. "Love," he whispered. "Love is the only thing that lasts...it's what makes the magic real. And, it's what Davis doesn't have."

"Ruth said something about love, too." Without realizing it, her arms were around him. "So, all the ideas Davis has about immortality are wrong?"

"Philip failed. And, yet Grace lived." Bob said, closing his eyes in the sudden rapture of his desire for Karen.

"Your grandmother Grace?" Karen asked.

"No; the little one," Bob said. easing Karen off his chest. "They were never the same person--though they are connected. As long as little Grace was cared for, everything stayed on an even keel. Her well being kept evil at bay."

"But, I killed her," she said.

He nodded. "Yes, you told me that. She was so weak and sad, and always feared that it would be her personal hell," he said as his hands took hold of her. "You saved her, Karen," Bob said, refusing to look into the eyes that always made his heart skip beats of anticipation. *I've said too much.*

"So, now what happens?"

"You've heard the saying--*all hell breaks loose?*"

"Are we here to face hell," she asked. He nodded. "Did Davis learn about the little people from Philip?"

I shouldn't involve you, his mind screamed. But the story fell out of his mouth like crumbs of bread. "I don't know if he even knew or, perhaps, found out. The Inn was built a long time ago. People had to be kept away from the woods. Sometimes a traveler came through the area and had to spend the night; the Inn was a safe place for them to stay."

Karen stared into his eyes.

"Dundury is a very dangerous place."

"And, your Grandmother started it all?"

"No, my grandmother Grace tried to help the man in the woods."

"And that man was Sherman, who played in the woods

and saw some evil." Her sarcasm dripped from every word. "So, the Kittendorf's must protect everyone until forever."

"You don't believe me," he said mournfully.

She reached up and gently touched his cheek. "Oh, Bob...I'm trying," she said, looking into his doubting eyes. "Really." She kissed his cheek. "Help me to believe."

His heart pulsed inside his chest as he held her gaze; if only he knew how she really felt about him. "My father was the only son in his family who was told the secrets of the little people."

You're part of all this...and you deliberately put me into the middle of it all... Tears spilled out of her eyes. "How could you do this to me?"

He wanted to pull her into his arms and tell her everything, but he dared not--not now. "Davis called and asked for my help. Bertha called you and--well, you're right. I sent you down here because--because I thought an article would help you, and an article would help Davis," he said, perspiration rolled down his face. "I knew something was wrong when I didn't hear from you," he said, pacing around her.

"And you think Davis has found a way to live," she said.

"Maybe." His heart pounded as he resisted telling her the truth.

"Did I start something when I--killed Grace?"

He abruptly stopped in his tracks. "No. Davis is the cause of all the knowledge leaking out."

"Why is he so fixated on Sherman? Why that time in history?"

"He claims Sherman spared Dundury because he had learned about the little people when he first visited in 1844. It's also the time his family learned the secrets. He's tried to build facts to support his claim, but none of it is true."

Karen remained silent, contemplating his words.

"Walk to the woods with me," he said, taking hold of her

hand. "My car isn't far." His arm moved to her waist again; she didn't discourage it. When they had reached his car, he lifted her up onto the hood. "Now listen--"

"I'm all ears."

"Kittendorf and Grace were the grand couple of Dundury. The little people were a part of the Kittendorf heritage that went back for generations in Ireland"

"You sound like Davis."

He rolled his eyes, rebuking the thought. "Little people inhabited our world. It's not known whether we came before or after them."

Karen held her silence; her gaze fixed on him.

"Are you listening to me?"

"Yes," she said in a near whisper.

"But you don't believe--do you?"

She shook her head.

"You held Grace in your hand. How can you not believe?"

What was it that Mignon said about prayer and magic, she thought, searching the jumble of things she'd been told.

"Karen!"

She shook her head again, this time trying to shock her senses back to the now.

"The little people have been around forever."

"Merlin could have made them," she said through a grin.

"Now, look who's sounding like Davis," he said, lowering his head in the futility of trying to make her believe.

"You said that your grandmother had wandered away..." She placing her hand under his chin and lifting his head. "Why are you so afraid to tell me?"

A tear betrayed him. This beautiful woman had filled his heart for so long. *Maybe-- against all I've been told and all that I've been trained for-- maybe it is time to share the secret.* Doubt guarded his words . *Maybe, this is how grandmother felt before the worst happened to her.*

She withdrew her hand from his face. "You're not going

to tell me," she said with finality. "You put me here."

"I never meant for any of this to happen...or for any harm to come to you...what a fool I was." His whispered words carried so much guilt. He forced a swallow that thundered in his head. "Father knew the evil had been unearthed."

"Because Grace was the last?"

He could only shrug his shoulders.

"Dammit, Bob! Tell me!"

"More will come--and so will the evil." He began to pace, only once glancing at Karen, then stopped and stood before her. "The year was 1844. My father was dying and my grandmother Grace was desperate to save him. When Philip offered to help her, I guess she thought--well, never mind. I don't know what she thought. She realized that she never should have confided in Philip; his actions confirmed the evil he sought. Everything Philip had touched turned bad; his crops died, the barns filled with cotton all burned to the ground...and his wife died in childbirth. It was horrible; they say the baby was terribly deformed."

Karen was speechless.

"Evil took possession, affirming Philip's lust for power," Bob said. "And Philip paid the price."

"How do you know these things?"

"My Father told me," Bob said, realizing that Karen hadn't believed him when he first tried to explain. "My Grandmother Grace and my Father began to change. It was strange. Something had taken hold of their souls, as if possessing them. Grandmother's bloodcurdling screams echoed through the trees as she tried to reach her beloved Kittendorf." Bob studied the look in Karen's eyes. *She doesn't believe me,* he told himself.

Bob continued. "Being a Protector was the only thing that saved him after my Grandmother vanished--without a trace-- never to be seen again."

Karen's face paled in his revelation. Her heart pounded an

intensity that made her breathing difficult until, finally, her breath caught. "Grace's husband--your grandfather-- is your *father*?" She began to tremble.

"I know how bizarre that sounds. But, it's true. I thought you understood when we spoke--"

"Your Father has lived..." she paused to do the mental calculation. "He's lived one-hundred-seventy-five years?"

Bob nodded.

"And, what happened to Philip?" Karen asked.

"Philip was consumed in his own curse. It began with his body... with uncontrollable shaking and trembling. Large welts popped up on the soles of his feet, then slowly covered his legs, until his entire body became one massive water-filled welt. The two little girls who lived here in Dundury to learn the magic had told everybody that the sores began first in Philip's soul."

Karen remained silent, her blank stare fixed to his eyes.

"He was in an ungodly agony; each sore burning and festering like a smoldering flame, a dying fire that refused to be extinguished. The girls had said that the smell of his burning flesh was horrific. It was hell itself," Bob whispered through a mournful voice. "It was during the worst of it when the little woman appeared. My Father named her Grace, in honor of his wife."

Karen edged closer to him.

"He loved my Grandmother."

"And was it a quick death for Philip?"

"No, it lasted all through the night until sunrise. The bowels of hell spit up its venom, forbidding any intervention. They could only watch, smell, and remember." Silence overtook Bob as his eyes glazed to everything around him.

"Hey," Karen said, tugging his sleeve. "Let's go. Let's just get in the car and get out of here."

"We have to see this through to the end."

"See *what* through," she said defiantly. "Everything

you've told me *is* bizarre--preposterous is more like it! And, yet, I believe you. Don't ask me why I believe you, I'm sure I can't give you an answer," she said through a hint of a smile.

"We have to stay."

Karen's arms wildly cut through the air. "Am I supposed to watch Davis have a melt down in front of me?"

Bob shook his head as he opened the passenger door for her. "I have to go check on Mignon."

"It's finished if we leave--it ends when we leave!" she yelled out, standing beside the car as he walked to the driver's door, opened it and slid behind the steering wheel, fastened his seat belt, then turned the key in the ignition.

Nothing happened.

Karen leaned into the car. "Don't tell me--*magic* has taken over," she said sarcastically.

"No, it's more like a lack of gas."

"You didn't know you were running out of gas?"

"Well, it was chugging a little when I stopped. I was damned glad I had enough to get here. I didn't think about getting back."

"That's why I love you, Bob," she said, shaking her head.

His lips parted in shock. "You do?"

"No, it was a joke. C'mon, let's just walk into the sunset like a couple of old fools." She slammed the door and started off down the road. She wasn't heading in the direction from which they'd come; she was struck out straight for the woods.

"You have any idea where you're going?" Bob called out to her.

"Yeah, away from you."

"That's just great," he said, running after her. "I pour my heart out to you and you walk away from me in a snit." *Come to think of it, you're always in a snit about something.* Karen stopped abruptly; Bob plowed into her. "Sorry."

"I've been here."

"That's impossible."

"Yes. I came here with Mignon. There, a few feet ahead--beyond that marshy area is the stump," she said.

"What stump?"

"Where we put the humidor."

"What humidor?"

She turned around to him. "You sure you know as much as you think you do?" She looked skyward, mocking a prayer. "Never mind! Where did you say your grandmother ended up? Do you know where she is now?"

The expression on Bob's face told her that he didn't.

Karen shook her head. "Are you going to Mignon's house?"

"Yes," he said. "I told you I want to see her."

"But, you thought we were going to her house when we were in the cellar at the Inn."

"I haven't been here in a long time."

"All of a sudden you're out here looking for her?"

"Lisa told me to try to find you at Mignon's or Davis'."

"Is that why you came--to find me?" Karen took a step back. Standing with him no longer seemed safe. Shadows moved in front of her. Step by shallow step she backed away.

"You can't just wander off! This place is dangerous."

"I told you, I've been here before. I know the way to Mignon's," she called out over her shoulder. Distance grew between them as her gait became a jog. *I can get there*, she thought. *But, is that where I want to be?*

Ava Lindsey Chambers

Chapter 9

A sound--no, it was more like a moan--seized Bob's senses. A moaning sound came from the opposite direction that Karen had gone. "Who's there?" Slow and careful steps drew him closer while he tried to muster his courage. "Davis?" he said, as darkness closed in around him. "Is that you, Davis?"

Davis responded, in a voice that was raspy and weak, "It is I."

"What are you doing out here?"

"I've been here all night. I can't seem to get my legs back under me," he said as Bob knelt down to him. Davis rolled his thumb over the fluted cylinder of the cigarette lighter.

"You look like hell. What happened?"

"I took a walk," Davis said. "I tried to get to Mignon's." The gasping sound that Davis made as he tried to breathe was frightening. "Somehow, I ended up here."

"I'll go get some help."

"No." Davis grabbed hold of Bob's sleeve. "I kicked this old stump for a long time, but I reckon the stump won. Turns out it's a good place to rest my head."

"Is it ending?"

"Yeah, and I'm...I'm glad you're here, Bob. You're the only friend I have."

"What happened to us, Davis?"

"I got her here for you, didn't I?"

"No, I believe she was sent," Bob said.

A small laugh exited Davis with great difficulty. "Well, I kept her here."

"Scared her half to death," Bob said. "Why'd you have to let her see Grace?"

"Grace needed to be released and I'm not sorry about what happened to her."

Bob inched closer to the stump. "She could have lived longer. Everything was set," he said, choking on the swell of emotion that caught in his throat. "Lisa had everything taken care of."

"I know what it's like to wait for death, to long for it's coming. Grace was ready. And, it's now my time," Davis said.

"Why? Because you wish to be dead? You know what happens when a little one dies."

"Your father started this mess. He got Mignon stirred up, reminded her of the prophecies," Davis said through a long gasp. "Once Grace was gone, I figured it would be over."

"All the clothes fit Karen, didn't they," Bob said.

"That's how I knew she was the one," Davis said, nodding. "I hosted all those damned historical meetings hoping to find someone who'd fit the clothes."

"Bertha must have known," Bob said, reflecting on the old woman. "It's why she sent Karen. And, poor Mignon thinks that fire will bring her death."

"It was predicted," Davis said.

"All that has happened was predicted," Bob said, his temper warming to the present threat. "Someone to fit our great, great grandmother's clothes... little ones dying," he said, standing and glaring down on Davis. "And, there's more-- much more to come. What about those Lucifer's?"

The manufactured grin returned to Davis' face. "Nice touch, don't you think? I found out about them by accident, saw 'em in a museum and had some reproduced."

"You're crazy. How did you know about the purging fire? Did my Father tell you?"

"I know all about fire. It's part of mankind. Every culture I visited had some kind of fire god."

"You think it purges," Bob said. "What about consuming fires?" he asked, staring at his friend. Little remained of the beautiful specimen he had once envied. "That's what Mignon fears," Bob said, shoving his hands into his pockets. "None of that matters now, Davis. It's all gone wrong. Father is out here somewhere."

"You'll have to find him. Mignon won't give up the magic." Davis' eyes slowly surrendered the battle to stay open.

"She won't help you, Davis."

"No. I guess I'll just sit here until I expire. Don't worry. I don't feel any pain, just a letting go."

"Stop being so damned melodramatic. I never liked it. I've got to find Karen--and my Father."

"My part is done...to a better place I go," he said.

Bob grabbed Davis' shoulders and shook him. "I can't do this by myself."

"I can't do anymore here," Davis said.

The crack of a twig sounded like a firecracker. "Oh my God, I forgot. Karen. What if she heard us?"

A laugh, evil and maniacal, rolled off Davis' lips. "A fine mess you're in, cousin," he said. "Pull that little pill bottle out of my pocket. I think I've got two left."

Bob searched for the medication. "I need to talk to Karen. I'll get some help for you. I won't leave you here for another night." Davis fell silent. Bob shook him, but Davis had fallen unconscious. "Please God, let Karen be far away from here."

The prayer was offered too late. Disgust flew all over Karen. There was no one to trust, no one to whom she could turn. *I've got to get to Mignon; she needs to know how close Davis is to unleashing the evil.*

She had wandered in the woods half the day and, now, it was nearly dark. She stopped, realizing that she was shivering and, suddenly, terribly confused. Bizarre and mysterious sounds whistled through the trees. Off in the distance, coming from opposite directions, traces of light seemed to beckon to her. One would be Ruth, and rest. The other would be Mignon, and only God knew what was in store for her there.

Faint footsteps sounded behind her, and then, the words leaked out. "Who's there?" Karen turned and began a slow canter toward the light--and Mignon--confident that the path she was following was the one she had been down only days before.

Lisa straightened Mignon's keepsakes, busying herself and trying to think of a reason to stay. Guilt filled her heart. She'd come back to her grandmother's birthplace hoping to find a simple, unencumbered lifestyle. Teaching had been an honor until the stories began. A lesson as simple as Snow White gave rise to the children of Dundury writing their own tale; each child reciting the same story.

The replica in her home had been a treasured family heirloom. Davis had been the most desirable bachelor in the county. Life had been easy, comfortable, routine. Then Grace came into her care. "Mignon?"

"Yes, child."

"What's going to happen?"

"Life will move on, as always."

Lisa turned to Mignon. *How can she be so calm?* There was no way Mignon didn't feel the thickness in the air. "Will it all be forgotten?"

"You can't forget what you don't know."

"Why do you always speak in riddles?"

Mignon remained silent.

"Can't you give me a straight answer-- Ever?"

The folds of Mignon's great purple dress appeared to float about her as weathered hands calmed the fabric that glided across the chair. "You got away from Kittendorf," she said.

"It wasn't difficult. He didn't really need me."

Mignon nodded. "You must leave me, my child."

"Yes, I suppose it's time to go. I've done all you required, haven't I?"

Again Mignon nodded. "Someone is coming, one who needs to go with you."

Lisa flipped the switch for the porch light, never noticing the odd smell of electricity, or the quick pop that the flipping switch had made. She stepped onto the porch. "Who's there?"

"It's me... Karen."

"Thank God," she said, grabbing Karen and pulling her in a frenzy; it stole all the confidence Karen had managed to collect. "Mignon said we need to leave here."

"I'm all for that," Karen said, nodding a greeting to the old woman. "Bob is out there with Davis. He couldn't get up. We should call someone."

"Come, child, sit for a minute and tell me."

As if a queen had summoned her, Karen had no will to refuse Mignon. "They're in the woods, by the stump." Mignon's brow lift. "They don't know," Karen said.

"Know what?" Lisa asked.

"They don't know..." Mignon said, preoccupied in thought. "That's why Davis is so weak. He's too near them." She leaned close to Karen. "Who else is out there, child? Did you see anyone else?"

A cold shiver passed over Karen, then moved to Lisa. Both crouched close to Mignon. "I heard something," Karen responded. "I don't know if it was a person or not."

Silence overcame the space as Karen and Lisa listened, waiting for an answer, or the hint of one.

The chair creaked as Mignon shifted her weight. Magic and mystery were illusions that had begun to wear thin. "Lisa," Karen whispered. "I've had enough. We need to leave Mignon in peace. Let's go."

"Yes, child," Mignon said, "Only one more visitor before I can go home, too." Her final words were lost on the two young women.

Lisa grabbed her purse and dug for her keys.

"I'm getting out of here tomorrow."

"What about Bob?"

A long sigh escaped Karen. "I guess I'll face him back in Marietta."

"You'll be all right?" Lisa asked Mignon.

"Don't forget to mail my package," the old woman reminded her.

Lisa nodded.

"Goodnight," Mignon said as the two left. A long exhale came with the finality of the closing door. "Good bye, child," she whispered.

Chapter 10

Lisa waited until Karen got into the car. "You're saddened by all that you've learned--aren't you," Lisa asked, turning the key in the ignition.

Karen lay her head back on the headrest. "I don't know what I've learned, or what I can believe."

"I came here looking for a quiet life, maybe a husband. I remember hot summers, cool green grass under bare feet, and love. There was love everywhere. Neighbors could be counted on to help. The people here were so close. It wasn't until I came back, as an adult, that I realized all was not as it had seemed."

"Because of the secret?"

"Yeah, more secrets than I ever imagined. What I thought was our family home, wasn't." Lisa shrugged. "Then Davis showed up. I thought he was interested in me. I was so wrong."

"Was Grace always in the house?"

"No, Davis brought her. 1 don't know how he found her."
Lisa paused and wiped the tears from her eyes. "I was
honored to have had Grace in my home."

"Were you able to talk to her?"

"Oh, yes. She was extraordinary company. I always
thought Davis was a bit jealous of our friendship. He wasn't
kind to Grace."

"What do you mean," Karen said.

"He badgered her, asking her all kinds of questions."

"What kind of questions--exactly," Karen turned to Lisa.

"Davis was part of a bad time. He and Bob were the best
of friends until they were ten, I think. Then Bob was sent off
to be cared for by a companion, and Davis was left with
Mignon."

"I guess that's when Bob moved to Marietta. He lived one
street over from us. Bob and my brothers were friends."

"Did you know his mother?"

"No... and I don't ever remember him mentioning her.
Bertha cared for him."

"That's the companion," Lisa said.

"My brothers used to spend a lot of time at Bob's house."

"I assume that Kittendorf wasn't around either?"

"I never saw him." *How could I know so little about
Bob?*" Only Bertha, with all her strange habits and
eccentricities."

"I've spoken to her."

"What did you think of her?"

"Oh, I don't know. I..." Lisa suddenly swerved the car,
narrowly missing an animal that darted into their path.

Karen panted as she came forward on the seat.

"That looked like a cat," Lisa said.

Karen's heart pounded. "I thought so too, a calico cat."

"There are no cats in Dundury. They eat the little people."

It was Karen's turn to shudder. "I have a little calico," she
said, staring down at her lap. "She's all I have now."

Dundury

Lisa turned into her driveway. "What about your family?"

"A drunk killed them in a head-on collision."

"I'm so sorry," Lisa said, turning off the ignition.

"Bob was a great comfort to me. We were close for a while." She sniffled. "I reminded him about how I wanted to be a writer."

"And he told you about Dundury?"

"No," Karen said, reaching for the handle. "He never said a word about Dundury until a few days ago," she stared at Lisa. "How was your family part of it?"

"I found what I thought was our family Bible. It had withered pages, faded pictures, and fanciful stories," Lisa said. "There wasn't any family information, which I thought was strange." She reached for the door handle. "I almost decided it was worthless."

But?" Karen asked.

"It was weird. When I tried to read it, the pages blurred and faded together. I took the book to school with me and used it to do a lesson on storytelling. It sparked such creativity in my children. They started telling *me* stories--all about Dundury--and all were the same."

Each woman closed their own thoughts until Lisa opened the door.

"Did Grace tell the same stories, too?" Karen asked.

"No, she talked about everything else. She did have one favorite story though...about some guy named Norman who had the war disease."

"*War disease?*"

"Yes. He was wounded in the War Between the States and became addicted to morphine. It was a story Davis loved to hear." Lisa smiled. "She told me how he always asked for cornbread, even when he had several pieces on his plate. Grace told the story so often. She truly loved that old man."

"I'm so numb to it all," she said shaking her head. "Why did it all happen?"

"My grandmother said that when a rule of magic was broken, there had to be consequences. Mignon doesn't believe that. To her, the time of the little people is over--just like the dinosaurs came and went. We all have our turn."

"Come on," Karen said. "Let's go in."

"Good idea," a voice from the back seat responded. "The conversation is mighty deep."

Lisa whirled around. "Kittendorf! Karen, get out! Run! Hurry!" She leaped out of the car, hitting the lock button as Karen slammed the car door. Together they raced to the house, pushed their full weight against the side door, and slid the bolts into their holding spaces.

"We're not safe, Lisa. There are other ways to enter this house."

Fear covered Lisa's face as she stood quaking in her shoes. The little house stood inches from her feet; she kicked it with all the fury she had bottled up. With one blow, the structure crumpled in a puff of smoke. Purple gleams of light flowed through the dust moving about the room as a soft laughing sound danced from the rafters.

"Why did you do that?"

An eerie vibration resonated from an upstairs room. "Someone's opening the wardrobe," Lisa said, grabbing Karen's arm and pulling her back toward the kitchen. "I packed your things," she said, pointing to the suitcase in the corner; her purse sat on top.

Karen pulled free of Lisa. "Bring me that Bible, everything your grandmother wrote, and your students' stories. Bring *everything* you have." Karen sat in the chair where the darkness consumed her. "I'm not going anywhere."

"But, they're coming! Don't you hear the wardrobe? And, Kittendorf--" Lisa said, moving toward Karen. "You can't stay here."

Shadows covered Karen's face as sparkling purple dust drifted down upon her. "I'm waiting for whoever you think will show up. I'd like to be armed with knowledge, but if that's impossible," she spread her arms like great wings, shrugged her shoulders, and folded her arms over her chest.

"I don't think you get it," Lisa challenged

"You're right, but I intend to." Karen crossed one slender leg over the other.

Lisa disappeared. Sound suspended itself. No squeaks, no moans, no soft sighs or breathing could be heard. Darkness deepened the room punctuated with tiny glows of purple light.

The miniscule light rays began to glow brighter, until the room was bathed in an peculiar brilliance. Bob slowly descended the stairs; he was carrying a book.

"What have you done, Karen," his voice sliced the silence.

Lisa returned to the sound of Bob's voice.

"She's begun the legacy. Davis told me someone would come--someone who could do it," Lisa said, gesturing at the light that wasn't light at all. A swarm of little bugs each with glowing tails and flittering wings invaded the room.

"They're fire flies, come to do your bidding," Kittendorf yelled, beating on the window pane until it broke.

"Let him in, Lisa. I want to know the whole story."

Lisa went to the door and unbolted it. Kittendorf's cape glided on the current of air as he raced into the living room and knelt down beside Karen.

Lisa shot a look at Bob. "You'll need to see this, then," Lisa said, walking to the old marble topped chest; she pulled out a book that was wrapped in plastic and tied with a red scarf. It vibrated in her hands.

Lisa and Bob each placed their half of the book in Karen's outstretched hands. The flittering fireflies formed a circle around the four.

All was still, except for the gentle hum of the fireflies. Karen lifted the book, first turning it over, then upside down, marveling at the curiously bound book. A sort of leather stuck to what felt like wood. Long lengths of wiry purple yarn, the same hue as the dust that had come from Grace's little mansion, held the spine together. Time immortal clung to the pages, rearing its hoary head into the air.

Karen opened the book and turned to what should have been the title page. She'd hoped for some date to identify the age of the manuscript. There was none. Blank pages fell open, like a teasing clown who refused to give up his secret. Then she gasped.

"What a beautiful dragon--as if ready to ascend the skies to cloak the world."

Kittendorf, Lisa and Bob gathered close. Purple dust seeped from the place where the wound on Karen's hand had been. The light around them pulsed, growing stronger with each beat.

"Turn to page forty eight," Kittendorf offered.

Karen took note of the tiny numbers on the pages that were void of any print or image. She turned page after page, careful not to harm the delicate paper. On page forty-eight a faint poem appeared.

Son to father
Twice four to eight
Return to beginning
Before it's too late

An aura, as if a glowing flame, formed a border around the words as Karen struggled to decipher their meaning. She rubbed her palm.

Kittendorf grabbed her hand, lifting it for all to see. "She has the mark."

"It's a scar," Karen said. "Mignon doctored my hand."

"It's part of the prophecy," Kittendorf said. "The little ones remained in this house. That's why it was left untouched, unchanged."

"How do you know this, Father," Bob asked.

"Because I've held this same book. It shows you what you need to know, when you need to know it." He grunted. "All the clothes fit Karen. They spoke to you, didn't they?" He inspected her hand. "Look how the dust is attracted to your wound. It's the most important part of the potion. A shape is forming."

Karen pulled her hand out of his. "That's ridiculous! The faces on the wall in the bedroom aren't real. It's the knotty pine paneling that makes it look like faces."

"And your hand?" Kittendorf demanded.

"I cut my hand on the little house."

"Cut it on what house?" Kittendorf demanded.

"On the..." Karen paused as she pointed to where the little house once stood. "The one..." Her throat refused to release the words as they all gazed at the empty space in the middle of the floor.

The fireflies hovered closer, up and over they flew, first around Lisa, then Bob, around Kittendorf, and, finally, back around Karen. Specks of colored dust drifted from the book with the flurrying beats of the tiny wings. Each human waited.

"This is all ridiculous," Lisa whispered. "Open the window and get these bugs out of my house."

"No!" Kittendorf screamed, staring a penetrating look into Karen's eyes, as if willing her to continue. "Please, there must be something else. All the magic is escaping."

"Father, how can you want the magic to continue when you've worked to contain it all these years?" He lowered his gaze to the book. "And, you were right. It's killing Davis."

Kittendorf's huge hands seized hold of Bob's shoulders. "What do you mean? Where is he?"

"In the woods-- dying. I gave him the last of his pills and told Mignon to send for help."

"And, did she?" he growled.

"I assume so," Bob answered.

"You didn't wait?" he growled.

"No, I followed you, Father."

"You're the fool I always thought you to be. Why did you leave him?"

Fire flashed from Bob to his father. "You helped him, Father! You're the great protector," Bob said sarcastically "You always held the magic--or should I say, *tried* to. Mignon never bragged, never mentioned what you couldn't shut up about. Your constant blustering is what damned Davis, you, *and* me."

"I tried to help. Why do you think I went to Mignon?"

"Mignon couldn't help. Davis wanted me," Karen said. "He thinks I can save him."

"No!" Kittendorf thundered, turning his weary face to her. "He wants what you have. The dust from the house, from the book, it's the last bit of magic. It can open up the world, destroy it, or become all that's left to save it. And..." he paused, then began in a whisper, "It's all going to you."

Karen glanced first at Bob, then back to Kittendorf. "I don't understand."

"Look at your hand. The color is there. The magic--it's there."

"No! Father, *please!*"

"It is too late. Mignon already buried Grace. If we could only find out where, maybe we could stop what is seeping out."

"The stump, they're buried in the old stump. Davis was right beside it," Karen said.

Kittendorf grimaced. "That would be why he was there. Somehow he must have felt an attraction to it. The lure to you was for the same reason. You have the same power inside."

"That's ridiculous," Karen said.

"Is it? Look at your hand."

"I hurt my hand, nothing more. I came to do a story. I wanted to write and Bob was helping me. Davis wanted a little publicity about the Inn, and Bob was helping him."

"No, dear lady," Kittendorf said. "It is much more than a story about an Inn."

"What about me?" Lisa cried. "Davis was so warm to me."

"You spent time here when you were growing up," Kittendorf told her. "I suspect Davis thought you possessed the secret he had searched for his entire life."

"But--" Lisa stuttered.

Kittendorf held up his hand. "You did find the book," he said, pointing to Karen's lap. "You just didn't know the power of what you had."

Karen looked at each face. "So this is all some elaborate plan Davis concocted?"

"Yes," Kittendorf said. "Davis needed a *special* power and you're it."

"What about the house he built? The little replica sat front and center."

"Davis helped build a lot of little houses around here," Bob said. "He loved the story, the history, and I believe he thought it might help bring tourism here to Dundury."

"Why would he care if he's dying?" Karen didn't miss the implication.

"He doesn't want to die, Karen," Kittendorf said. "He wants the answers--the incantation."

Her brow punctuated curiosity. "Why?"

"Because he's part of the prophecy. But Davis can *never* --under any circumstance--learn the magic. It would mean the end of all life," Kittendorf said in a voice filled with sadness. "Philip was my uncle who pretended to love my mother in an attempt to learn what was forbidden. He felt it had been denied him."

"And Philip is Davis' great-grandfather." Karen said.

"No--his prodigy, one might say." Kittendorf nodded, reluctant to give up the long-hidden truth.

"So, Davis wants what Philip could never have," Karen

said with finality. Neither Bob nor his father responded. She sensed the tension between the two men.

Bob stared into space. "I want you to tell me what happened to my mother," he finally said, without looking at his father.

"That's a story that will have to wait for another time." Kittendorf tried to be gentle. "Right now, I want to find Davis. I just pray he is alive and with Mignon." He stood up and headed for the front door. An horrific gasp escaped him as he opened it.

"Good grief, it's the cat," Lisa said, moving to the door.

"A cat-- In Dundury?" Kittendorf gasped.

"It's a little calico," Karen said, reaching to stroke the creature. "It looks like the one I have back home."

"Cats don't belong around here," Bob said.

"It's a sign," Kittendorf said. "A very bad sign. We must hurry."

Bob hesitated. "You don't need me, I'm not part of this. I inherited no magic, no power."

Kittendorf turned. "You have the greatest power of all, son. You have a good and loving heart. You must reach Davis." He touched his son's arm. "Please...we all have to do this together." The open door offered the dark of night. The tiny fire flies exited before them and the cat leapt off the porch.

Chapter 11

Lisa followed after the cat. "Kitty, kitty," she called, stepping through the light dew on the grass, and moving along the side of the house. "Come here, little kitty."

Kittendorf frowned an irritated look as he glanced back at the front door. "Where's Karen?"

Bob turned around. "I thought she was right behind me."

"Well, go get her. We will finish this tonight." The authority in his voice left no room for hesitation.

Bob ran back into the house. "Karen, where are you? We've got to go," he said, nearly knocking her off her feet.

"I'm bringing my things, taking my car, and leaving in the morning. Whatever is to happen, will happen tonight."

The hair on the back of his neck stood on end. How could he ever make her understand the strangeness of his existence. *I've known you nearly my whole life...*he thought, acutely aware that his heart longed to include her in his world in a way that would bind her to him forever. Distrust of him and his intentions was the barrier between them.

"Earth to Bob," she said, tapping his forehead. "Will you help me with my things, please?"

To answer was too difficult. Curt and distant was easier. *Karen has no idea what she's about to face.* He picked up her suitcase and followed her out the front door.

Karen felt a tingling through the scar on her hand, a feeling that moved throughout her whole body. Never had she experienced the sense of being so alive. The secret of Dundury was part of Bob and his family. What else lay hidden inside her friend? *Friend,* Karen thought; an odd word, considering all that they'd been through.

"I'm ready," she said, following him across the porch. "Where's Lisa?"

"She's after the cat." Kittendorf said.

Bob looked at his father. "You said it was a bad sign."

"We've got to get rid of it." Kittendorf said.

"No," Karen said, her voice rising in horror. "It's an innocent--"

"It's as innocent as a snake in the grass," Kittendorf snapped. "Cats killed most of the little people in the world. A calico is the worst, she soaks up the colors of magic, so that people forget."

"Get in the car and leave the cat alone," Karen ordered. "Bob, you come with me," she said heading toward her car. "Kittendorf, find Lisa and bring her. And, I don't want to hear anymore about cats."

A low whistle came from Kittendorf. Only Bob knew how serious that sound could be. He had never seen his father give in, and he wasn't now. The air hung heavy with evil.

Karen backed through the grass, maneuvering the car around Lisa's. The car rolled over the curb and hit the street with a bounce.

"Lisa, come on," Kittendorf called out. "They're leaving."

Lisa came running, then tried to unlock her car.

"Well," Kittendorf demanded in a voice bare of patience.

"I... I guess you're coming with me," Lisa said, nervously and dropped her keys.

"So it would seem," Kittendorf said, motioning for her to get in the car. "Can you hurry, they're getting ahead of us."

Flashes of lightning illuminated the sky. Karen wished for the little fireflies and the curiously strange feeling of hope that they brought to her.

"Did your father live with you when you were little?"

He shook his head. "Father came once in a while. I was raised by the companion I always thought my mother had chosen for me."

"You mean, Bertha?"

He shrugged, then turned to the window and the darkened night.

"So, it was kind of like being adopted?"

"In a way, I guess," he said.

"And, Davis was left in Dundury?"

"Yes, it was considered the safest way at the time."

"Safe for whom?" Karen asked.

"For everybody," Bob said, turning to face her.

"Why?"

"So the magic wouldn't leak out again."

Splats of rain hit the windshield. Karen slowed the car to a crawl and maneuvered a quick turn onto the side road. "Is Davis the cause of all this?"

"I don't know. He gave me the idea to start the magazine. He even sent some seed money. A few years passed, then he called a few days ago with his grand idea to turn Dundury into a tourist mecca. The little people, the old South-- it had all the ingredients for success. He wanted my help and...I owed him that much," Bob said, rubbing his neck.

She saw the perspiration on his forehead.

"I started getting threats. Notes showed up on my desk. Somebody was reminding me that the little people were protected, the secret had to be guarded," he said, looking into her eyes as she quickly glanced his way. "Then Kittendorf reappeared in my life-- and yours."

"He's not a part of my life."

"I found him watching you. I think he..."

The car swerved, almost sliding down the embankment and into the murky swamp that paralleled the road.

Lights behind them flashed a warning.

"For what reason?"

"Kittendorf is a protector--a protector at all costs."

"You already told me that--exactly what does that mean?"

"He was ordained to protect the secrets of the little people who keep evil at bay. I just never knew how far he would go."

"Could your father be after Davis?"

"I'm not sure. Lisa said that Davis began telling wild stories, it's part of the reason for his holding the historical meetings. He was always digging for information, the horrible stories of war, all the cruelty. She felt he was going mad."

"But you told me he was always like that."

"Only to a point. He loved history, especially Southern lore." Bob smiled. "He can tell you every campaign and all of Sherman's troop movements."

"If he knows about the evil," Karen mumbled. "Why would he want people to come to Dundury?"

Bob continued, not hearing a word Karen said. "He said he'd finally gotten title to some land and wanted to make Dundury a showplace."

*They'd learn about the little people...*Karen thought.

"I think Davis was hoping to redirect what was happening...that the truth was the best protection."

Lightning blazed across the sky; Bob continued. "I don't think he understood the totality of what could happen."

"It was already too late," Karen said. "The knowledge had seeped out; the power had been unleashed," she whispered.

Bob stared a curious look at her. "The curse has begun,"

he muttered under his breath.

Rain hit the windshield in a torrential downpour, stealing Karen's control as she inched the car down the road. She leaned forward over the steering wheel. "Do you see the turn?"

Bob twisted around on the seat to see the lights behind them, then turned back to the windshield. "On the right up there, I think." I wonder what Lisa and Kittendorf are discussing?" Lightening flashed. "There's the driveway, turn now," he said, pointing to his right.

"The house is dark," Karen said. "Maybe Mignon took Davis to the hospital."

"No, I don't think she drives. I wonder if she went out into the field to sit with him."

"If you know so much about Mignon, why did you think the Inn was her house?"

"It is her house, but she lives out here."

She pulled the car to a stop and angrily jerked the hand brake.

"We have to wait for the others." Bob said, looking out the rear window. "Here they come."

Karen waited as Lisa positioned her car. It blocked the path of retreat. "I don't like this. Something isn't right."

Kittendorf, oblivious to the rain, sauntered toward them. "Come on. I'm sure Davis is here." He walked to the front door, pushed the key into the lock, and opened it.

"He has a key!"

"All protectors have a repository of keys, Karen," he said, looking around. "Where's Lisa?"

"There she is," Karen said, pointing as Lisa disappeared down the path beside Mignon's house. "She must be going to the stump."

"In this rain? You think she can find it?" Bob asked.

"Let's check on Mignon."

They found Kittendorf standing inside the living room.

Mignon was nowhere to be seen. Bob and Karen approached the burly old man as something scampered across the threshold.

"What was that?" Bob asked.

"It's a cat," Karen said. "I don't think calico she wants us to go inside."

Kittendorf's black boot suddenly kicked the cat.

"Why do you have to be so mean?" Karen sneered.

"It's his way, child," Mignon's voice said from a corner in the darkness.

Karen stepped over the cat and into the house. "Mignon, thank God," she said. "Where are you, Kittendorf?"

"I'm here." His voice drifted from the shadows. "Davis is in the back. He's still alive."

"Follow me to the white bedroom," Karen said. With each step that brought her nearer to Davis, the more her hand throbbed. Waves of electricity traveled from her palm, up her arm, and directly to her heart. She staggered, grabbing hold of the bedpost.

Davis opened his eyes. "Touch me, Karen. Please, end this torture," he pleaded. His face was flushed, but it was the strange odor that repulsed her. She hesitated, noticing the open sores on his face.

"Touch him. If Father is right, you will save him," Bob said.

"Who put the curse on you, Davis?" Karen asked, not conscious of her choice of words.

Mignon's voice bellowed out: "I did!"

Karen felt a strange resistance like that of a magnet; it repelled her body with each step she advanced closer to the bed. She held out her arm, trying to touch Davis. "I can't. I don't have the strength. Mignon..." she yelled out, then fell to the floor beside the bed.

The voices were distant, yet demanding, as they drifted into her last moments of consciousness. A door opened and closed, and Bob rushed to her side.

"Kittendorf, I think I've found it," Lisa cried out as she burst into the house. "I found the humidor," she yelled, coming down the hall. "It's in the woods. I tried to get it out of the stump, but it wouldn't budge."

Lisa looked as if she had emerged from the grave. Bits of dirt and pine straw clung to her wet and matted hair. Her manicured fingernails were the color of clay. "Davis?" Her breath came quick and heavy. "Is he dead?"

"Cursed, just like the rest of his family," Mignon hissed, as she followed Kittendorf down the hall.

"But, the childrens' stories...There's help from..." Lisa paused, searching for Karen. Her eyes settled on Kittendorf. "Does Karen have the power?"

Kittendorf nodded. "Yes, she does."

"Then make her touch him," Lisa said. "Where is she?"

"Here," Bob said, and Kittendorf stepped aside as Bob lifted Karen into his arms. Her head fell against his shoulder as he brushed her hair from her face.

"Make her touch him," Lisa begged.

"The damn thing is guarding her," Kittendorf said, pointing down at the calico.

A gentle touch brushed the back of Bob's hand. The calico cat was licking Karen's face.

Kittendorf moved closer. The cat hissed her warning.

"Cats don't belong in Dundury," Bob whispered to the cat, remembering Bertha telling him about the long standing rule.

"Please, I burn!" Davis screamed, writhing in agony.

"Well, Kittendorf," Mignon said, moving from behind his great girth. "It seems I have won after all," she said. "My will, my curse, has become the strongest. You thought bringing another here would help. You've forgotten the simplest of rules."

The protector's respect evaporated as he grabbed

Mignon's arm and pulled her out of the room, the door slammed behind them. "You didn't see the tiny boxes of fire? And you don't see the jeopardy you're in."

Mignon stifled her smile. *Kittendorf, you're too weak to stop the power.* "What would you have me do?"

"Purging fire," Kittendorf said. "That's the prophecy, don't you remember?" He pushed her down the hall. "Fire is to be your end. You failed all eternity...you were to control Davis, but you failed. Instead, he searched until he found that which was to have been forever denied him."

"I did what I thought was best. I held sacred the teachings, Kittendorf," Mignon said. "And, now, it begins," she whispered, then sat down on her huge wing-backed chair, and spread out her great robe.

"Are you afraid?" Kittendorf said.

Silence was her response.

Lisa ventured a move beyond the cat. "Do you smell something," she whispered to Bob.

"I smell smoke." Bob stumbled to his knees, holding Karen in his arms. "You've got to wake up!" he said, hugging her. "There's no way out," he said to Lisa.

Panic began to overwhelm Lisa. Davis moaned. The cat hissed. Karen opened her eyes and tried to focus.

"Karen! Wake up! We've got to get out of here." Bob stared down at the cat as if daring it to interfere.

"We're trapped," Lisa screamed. "The smoke is getting thicker! I can't find the door! There's no way out!"

Karen pulled shallow breaths, choking as the smoke filled her lungs.

"Listen to me, Karen," Bob said. "When we were younger, I spent time with your brothers. We played knights of the round table. It wasn't just play, Karen. Remember how you always wanted to join us. Think of the magic... the valor, the knowledge that right always wins. It still survives, Karen," he said, begging her to remember.

Davis laughed through his pain. *"Valor?* There's no such thing," he hissed. "Only pain and death exist in this world. The little ones know it; it's what draws them out." A purple mist mixed with smoke as it seeped into the room.

"Karen, you've got to help us," Lisa cried, tears gushing down her face.

"There is a way out.," she choked her words. "I've been here before." Pain shot through her hand as she braced herself to stand.

Lisa moved closer and pulled Karen to the bed. *"Please!* Please touch him... save him, Karen!"

"The door is only visible to those who know where to look," Karen said, still choking her words.

Lisa struggled to lift Davis off the bed; the stench of him far worse than the smoke smothering them. Sores burst open, draining a gooey pus. His feet were as raw meat. The pain so intense, he hadn't the strength to move.

"You know the secret," Lisa screamed.

"Get out of my way," Karen yelled at Lisa, then reached for Davis and gently stroked his cheek. She turned and moved to the wall and the flowers. She touched the near invisible space. The door popped opened. Bob hoisted Davis over his shoulder. Davis screamed out in agony as Bob bounced off the door racing down the smoke-filled hall. He stumbled down the back steps, scarcely able to keep his balance, then rolled Davis off his shoulder and onto the ground. Lisa dropped to her knees beside Davis.

Bob ran back inside, frantically racing down the hall. "Karen! Where are you?"

"I've got to get the cat," she called out, half-staggering, half-crawling, back down the hall toward the white room. Voices echoed in a strange pitch. She fought the mist and smoke as she turned the corner to the living room. She saw Mignon sitting on the chair, imperious and disimpassioned, as the fiery mass burst forth, engulfing her.

Kittendorf had vanished. Questions and curiosity went unsated as the calico cat wound herself between Karen's legs, gently coaxing her steps backwards and away from the flames.

Karen tumbled to the floor, crawling back the way she'd come. The cat, ever close, stayed her course beside Karen.. Each time the cat touched her, an unknown, inexplicable strength seemed to flow from the cat and into Karen. Finally, they had reached the threshold at the back door and, smelling the sweet rainswept scent of fresh air, Karen reached for the soft fur. "You remind me of my other little friend."

"Karen!" Bob screamed. She heaved herself out the door, rolling to a stop at his feet.

Pink streaks of morning filled the sky. Air, precious and pure, filled lungs that had fought deprivation. "Mignon is dead," she said without emotion.

"Oh, my God! No!" Bob said, helping Karen to stand. A thunderous boom blew them backwards and off their feet as the house exploded.

"No one concerned about me?" The dark coat whipped around Kittendorf boldly standing in a Confederate hat which only intensified his frightening appearance.

"You started the fire hoping to kill us all," Bob snarled as the bile drew up in his mouth and, in one moment of intolerance, he spit at his father's feet.

"Mignon's dead," Karen stated flatly.

"But the fire didn't get you." Kittendorf's voice touched a nerve raw with emotion.

Karen lunged at him.

"You must not be angry, Karen," Kittendorf said.

"My feet," Davis cried out. "Lisa! Look at my feet!" He lay in the grass, his delicate fingers pointing down to his toes that began to wiggle and turn pink. "I can feel my feet again!" A smile threatened to show itself.

"Please touch him again, Karen. Your hand will do the magic. Please," Lisa begged.

The cat squirmed in Karen's arms as she moved toward Davis. Kittendorf moved with her. Each deliberately and slowly moving closer to Davis.

Kittendorf made a grab for Karen, the cat let out a menacing hiss and leapt at his face. Kittendorf swung his arm and the cat sailed into the air, then dropped to the ground with a deadening thud. The lovely feline lay still for a moment before racing off into the woods.

"Afraid of a cat, Kittendorf?" Karen whispered, momentarily forgetting Davis.

"She'll be our undoing," Kittendorf snarled.

Bob rushed at Kittendorf, his fists drawn, prepared to do battle with his father.

"Aim to hurt me, son?" Kittendorf said sarcastically. "You still don't know who I am."

Bob's back stiffened. "I don't care who you are. I know *what* you are--that's all that matters."

Tears fell from Karen's eyes, dripping into the sodden ground around the flames that billowed from Mignon's little cottage. "You're the one who did this," she whispered. "Evil does endure the ages, doesn't it, Kittendorf?"

"It's wise you are, Karen. While Bob remains oblivious and dimwitted, as always."

With hands tightly fisted, Bob ran at his father. Karen jumped between them, stopping the blow that threatened the old man's face. "Violence isn't the answer."

Kittendorf dashed into the woods.

Lisa struggled to help Davis to his feet.

"Help me," Davis said. "Kittendorf's heading for the stump. We have to stop him."

"You're in no condition to stop anything. It was you and your lust for magic that dragged us all into this," Bob said, steadying Davis. "And I've involved Karen."

"Mignon was part of it, too," Lisa said.

Bob turned to the smoldering embers of all that was left.

"Her work was done. Her time had ended," Karen said, glancing at Lisa. "Just as she said, '*we all have our time.*'"

"Maybe she *can* help us," Lisa offered.

"She won't help," Davis sneered. "She wants the power... Kittendorf wants the power... and maybe..." he squinted his eyes at Bob. "Maybe even you."

Shrieks and screams cut into the morning calm. The cries going beyond anything that had ever been heard on earth.

Bob began to sweat. "It's morning and it's still not over," Bob said, swinging around to Davis. "What next, Davis?"

"Go to the stump," he said. "The humidor holds what's important."

Bob and Karen ran for the stump. Lisa remained to help Davis; she saw the way his mouth twisted in a mocking smile and his eyes took on a malevolent look.

Chapter
12

The sounds in the wood grew stronger and stranger as Bob led Karen; and Lisa tracked behind them with Davis in tow. Slow, silent steps took them closer to the noises while the morning sun fell behind a cloud, leaving the world shaded in a purple mist.

I fear the night but dread this day more than any I have known, Bob thought, struggling to remember what he'd been taught about Dundury. *There was to be a time of evil and strife in the world*, he remembered his father had said *it is foretold*. But that had been Sherman's march to the sea, the fire that had consumed the South, thanks to the Yankee Sherman and his meddling in Dundury. Over a century had passed. What more could happen? *Fate has brought me to this place... a Fate which cannot be ignored*

A hissing sound drew his attention; his father's glare was penetrating.

Kittendorf ascended the small incline in front of them. He

stretched out his arms, his long black coat shielding everything in front of him. "Life eternal? But humans are too weak for that," he said, as if talking to someone. "Don't you see, dear Grace, I *can* stop it. I *will* end it."

A shriek answered his words.

"Who answers you, old man," Bob called out.

Kittendorf's arms reached upward. "I have all that is left." He spun around in a sudden fury and lifted his eyes to the sky. "This cannot--and will not continue!"

"What's he talking about?" Karen whispered in Bob's ear; Bob shook his head, his eyes intently focused on his father. She felt the clamminess of her silk blouse sticking to her wet skin.

Lisa came up behind them. "What's he doing?"

A run of liquid rolled down Karen's back. "It's so hot--"

Davis frantically pushed Bob and Lisa out of his way, reached for Karen and spun her around. His eyes scrutinized her as if she were a specimen in a petrie dish. "You're not blistering up yet... do you feel pain?"

Karen used the sleeve of her shirt to mop the sweat that covered her face. She reached for Davis. "Did you feel... hot and... nauseous before... before the blisters started?" she said, unsteady and swaying on her feet. Bob grabbed hold of her. "I feel like..." she gasped, pulling quick pulls of air. "Something's covering me..." she moaned. "It's squeezing."

"No, it wasn't like that at all," Davis said, shaking his head. "I just hurt all over."

"And, boy, did you stink," Lisa reminded him.

Bob eased Karen to the ground. "Kittendorf!" Bob screamed out to his father as Karen arched her back, desperately trying to pull air into her lungs.

Kittendorf ran down the hill. "I told you not to come, Bob. I told you," Kittendorf said, folding his arms and anchoring them over his chest. "I told you I'd know if you came," he said, moving in a graceful, even elegant way. He stopped short of the stump; and beckoned Bob and Karen to come closer. "The pit of hell beckons," he said, staring down at the dim, almost imperceptible glow that, moment by moment, grew in intensity as its radiance began to pulse like a heartbeat.

"It's where I lay days ago," Davis said, awestricken at the burning incandesce and vibrating earth.

"It's the stump where Grace... and Philip are buried," Karen panted, dropping to her knees before the stump. "Can you feel it?"

Lisa knelt down to Karen and wrapped her arms around her. "It isn't burning--it's glowing."

"Let me see your hand," Kittendorf demanded, lowering himself to one knee and reaching for Karen's hand.

"Leave her alone," Bob demanded, grabbing his father's arm.

"You know the predictions! The world will change *forever* if I don't do my part," Kittendorf snarled into his son's face. "I am the protector!" he screamed. "You will leave me to this... *before* the evil escapes."

"No!" Davis screamed, yanking Bob's hand free of his father. "Sherman understood the magic here in Dundury... he accepted his duty."

"Sherman was too weak to fight the evil that commanded him to spread it so abundantly throughout the South. He scorched the earth and desecrated the innocents! *That* is why the South can never forget--why it will forever mourn," Kittendorf said, glaring into their eyes. "It wasn't the *end of an era*, as the romantics have called it," he snarled. "It was the *beginning of the age of evil, lo these last hundred-and-fifty years--*" he paused, the ferociousness of his commitment confirmed in his eyes. "I will end it now."

"You stupid old fool!" Davis screamed. "It's the *power*...the *glory* the South has mourned."

"Shut up!" Bob grabbed Davis' arm. "You've lost all

perspective." *They haven't a clue how perilous their position is.*

Karen lay speechless, her soaking wet body trembling as she moaned in her desperate gasps for breath. Droplets of perspiration rolled down her neck and onto the dirt.

Kittendorf reached for her again.

Bob grabbed his arm again. "I told you to leave her alone."

Kittendorf's piercing black eyes slowly moved from Bob's hand, along his arm, up his neck, until his eyes seared his son's. Power rushed forth from the old man. Nothing would separate him from his mission. Hoots and squeals from the shadows buoyed his determination. "You are my son, but do not presume to think that you can stop me."

The pitch of Karen's voice penetrated the moment. "Bob! Oh, God--help me!"

"Fight, Karen!" Bob screamed, grabbing her up into his arms, seizing the evil that invaded her soul.

Kittendorf slugged Bob, knocking him back and off his feet. "The world will stop spinning. The clouds will overtake the sun."

"The time has come," Davis screamed jubilantly.

Tears dropped from Bob's eyes; he was losing her. "Karen!"

A thunderous roar vibrated the ground around them as snakelike hissing sounds and bloodcurdling death screams moved in around them. Succubus had called up his baneful winds and the purple mist drifted up from the stump-- cloudlike and ominous, engulfing them all.

"Death comes," Davis said. "Mignon told me that I made the wrong choice. The stupid old woman." His laugh was a grotesque sound of one possessed. "Power *will* win over faith, and power will *never* surrender to the weakness of *love*," he said, falling to his knees laughing at the insanity of his thoughts. "Woe is me," he wailed. "I should have listened to old Mignon. Tsk, tsk, she's gone but I'm not." Laughter bellowed out of him.

"Karen!" Bob cried out, chopping at the mist in a frantic search to hold onto her. "Remember the silly stories... how you wanted to be a fiction author and write great stories. This is one of those tales, Karen! It's just a mindless story... don't believe. *Please*, Karen, don't believe!"

Davis rolled back and forth across the dirt, his hands and legs flailing in the mist. "Karen, you must believe... believe, my love," he cried out.

Kittendorf's eyes were locked on Bob. "She doesn't love you enough, does she, son? You should have worked much harder, my boy. You were taught the *magic*! Remember it, boy, remember!"

"Karen, please," Bob begged. The shrieking sound had a new tone; low and distant and terribly mournful. Bob searched his memory for something that would save her. The cat. She always loved cats. *Would it be enough?* "Karen, remember little Calico...she waits for you. She needs you, as a child needs her mother."

In that instant, time had frozen and the brightness of the morning returned as Kittendorf sailed high above them, his arms outstretched, his cape fluttering on the wind. The empty sky, void of even clouds, suddenly lighted the heavens. The earth vibrated through the flashes exploding around him; as a thunderbolt hammered the stump.

Kittendorf and Karen were gone-- vanished into thin air.

Lisa stood crying. Davis slowly got to his feet, stifling his delight. Bob seemed transfixed, as if in another world

The heat was suffocating through the sense of falling while the sound of a rushing wind filled her ears, vibrating her brain into a useless mush. Words bounced inside her head, their meaning unclear and then, soft earth brought a cessation to everything.

A deep and penetrating cold, the likes of which she had never felt before, encased her wet body. She was helpless to stop shaking. She felt her eyes were open, but nothing came into focus, except an emerald veil.

The deadening quiet stole Karen's last nerve. *Alice fell into the rabbit hole, and Karen fell into the well. That's it,* she told herself. *I've fallen into a well. That's why I'm wet, and so cold and alone, and...*

The veil lifted and she saw the cavern walls and the hollowed-out openings in the walls that dampness and cold made glisten. She forced her arms to move around her, rubbing a friction that might stop the shaking that jarred every bone in her body.

"Bob... can you hear me?"

"I think we're in hell." Kittendorf's voice came as a whisper, near and yet, so far.

"Kittendorf?" Karen crawled to her knees.

"Yes, dear girl. It is I."

"How did you get here?"

"The same way you did."

"Where are we?"

"Hell," he answered.

"Hell would be dark," she said, refuting his words.

"What about the consuming fires?"

"I'm not going to hell!" she snapped.

"Are you so pure? So good? Or, did Mignon give you the secret that would save you?"

"I thought you knew everything, Devil."

Kittendorf laughed as he came walking out of one of the dark passageways. "I have a job to do." He rubbed the top of his head, just as Bob always did, and looked around the cavern. "I wanted to prevent this."

"Oh, please. You killed Mignon! You tried to kill me," she said, slowly standing up.

"No, Karen, I wanted you all to leave Dundury and its

evil," he said, quite sincerely with almost a hint of sorrow.

"If it was all predicted--how did you think you could stop it?"

"Perhaps, I can't. I am, after all, only mortal--as you."

"*Mortal*? You're one-hundred-seventy-five years old!"

"Yes, but mortal still. And you're here with me--aren't you?"

She nodded, still rubbing her arms for warmth.

"You're here because Bob thought the love of a cat would save you."

"What?"

"He learned from Bertha, a long time ago, that the only way to be saved was to find love."

"What do you know about love?" She challenged him.

"Love is the strongest of all God's gifts--and faith." Kittendorf forced his words. "Bob was trying to convince you that the love of your precious little calico cat would save you. He did that for a reason."

She didn't have an answer.

"Why would the stupid boy choose a cat?" Kittendorf grabbed a hold of her, forcing her to face him. "You do know that cats were the keepers of the underworld in Egypt... they are familiars and even help witches. How evil is that?"

"It's superstition," she countered weakly.

"Did you know that of all the animals mentioned in the Bible, the cat isn't one of them. Noah didn't even put one on the ark."

No, she didn't know any of that.

Kittendorf leaned into her face and grinned. "Bob knew you'd never love someone as pathetic as--"

"You think your son is pathetic?"

"I counted on it," Kittendorf said, lowering his head. "It would have kept him safe from the evil that seizes men's hearts, from the force that drives us all into oblivion."

Anger and fear welled up inside her; she had to get away

from him if only the muck she was standing in allowed it. Still, each gulping backward step kept her within his realm.

"Not making much progress, are you?" Kittendorf said.

Each dogged step reinforced her determination. *How could light appear to be black*, she wondered, staring at the intense purple glow surrounded by the green haze that grew larger as her slow steps moved her closer--to what? Suddenly, something moved in the mist.

"Kittendorf--is that you?" *Has he found another way around me? Or, is there something else here?* Again, the gurgling sound of something stepping in the murky mass halted her. "Who's there?" Another squishing step stole another ounce of her courage. "Kittendorf," she whispered. "Where are you?"

"I'm behind you," he answered.

"Did you see something move?"

"It can't be," he said as incredulity choked him in silence.

The bewildering light began to entrance her. "Where are you?"

"Still behind you. It's the searing flame of evil!" His words stopped her dead in her tracks.

Mist drifted over them. A shriek made her jump while fear tightened her throat.

The mist grew heavier and, with it, came heat. At first Karen welcomed the warmth that made her shivering stop and her body begin to dry. Hope returned, but only momentarily. As she rubbed her arms, she felt a grainy substance. The sweat had crystallized. The heat grew more intense and unbearable. The purple haze slowly acquiesced to the green darkness. And, with it came a strange and enticing scent that lured them deeper into the cavern.

"Look!" She shouted, moving forward.

"What is it?" Kittendorf asked, pushing past her. "The scent is marvelous. It seems to be coming from over there, from some sort of orb." His raspy voice grew young and playful, and he pulled off his coat and laid it on the dirt floor before her. "Kneel on my coat."

She obliged him. "It's cooler over here. C'mon," she said crawling to the edge of his coat.

Kittendorf stood up. "It glows, Karen. It's beautiful."

Just beyond his coat, she reached out and touched the surface of the cave. The coolness of it felt wonderful. She crawled closer. "The floor--it's copper." She tried to remember. "The humidor was lined with copper. The heat-- it turns copper green if you do something to it. But the humidor had to be moist, that's why there's water," she said, trying to understand the mystery of the thing before her.

"Such great knowledge you have," said a voice that vibrated her head.

Karen turned. The cave was empty. Only Kittendorf's coat was proof that he had abandoned her. Panic forced her to her feet. "Kittendorf?"

"He is gone. A protector never removes his coat."

Ava Lindsey Chambers

Chapter 13

The fragrance permeated the cavern. Karen struggled to stand; she felt Kittendorf's coat sliding beneath her feet.

"Karen," The voice was pleasing, almost seductive as it spoke her name.

"Who's there?"

"The one you seek," it said, oozing seduction that caressed her skin, tantalizing her senses as it whirled around her.

"I'm not seeking anyone."

"What is it you yearn for?"

"I don't know...a good story...a big break. I don't know."

"What is it you miss?"

"My family," she said, until anger bit her senses. "What business is it of yours?"

"What is it that you'll do?"

"*Do?*"

"Yes, and what will you do for your success...your family," the sultry voice said, hoping for fulfillment.

Her senses wandered in the the maze of emotions that took hold of her. Her saving grace was the horrific scream that pierced her senses. "Somebody's hurt!"

"No."

"Then why the agonizing cries?" she asked.

"Lost," the bewitching whispered voice said.

The intoxicating aroma invaded her senses again. "I'm gonna find out what's happening."

"If you dare."

"What are you?"

"Kittendorf told you that Evil resides here."

"To hell with you!" Karen shouted, forcing her leg to take one more step in the sucking muck. The sleeves of Kittendorf's coat tangled around her ankles, as if discouraging her. Eerie lights gleamed somewhere in the distance. Screams crawled the walls until they surrounded her.

"You're a strong one," were the words that meant to buoy her self-confidence. "But, I will win," the voice taunted her.

"I don't know who or what you are--and I don't care!"

"Oh, but you do care, Karen," the voice persisted, its sound enveloping her head, taunting her ears as a lover's tongue. "All of life is a game, Karen. And, you so love the challenge."

Karen shook her head. "You're much too obvious, demon," she said, taking another step and staggering headlong into the cavern wall. Her palm slid off of something sharp; a hot pain shot through her palm, and up to her shoulder. The wound glowed bright in the darkened cave. As if by instinct, she held her hand out in front of her, using it as a light. She headed toward the screams, stepping through congealed mush.

"Aaaahhhhh..." resounded off the walls of the cavern; the mournful wails gave no evidence of either a human or animal source.

Her steps became easier as the ground grew firmer. Warmth gave way to heat, and heat to dryness. A sense of remembrance came through the ages. Her palm glowed brighter, and the pain ceased. Weakness fell away as she stood tall; her confidence had returned. And then, she slipped.

Her own shriek melted into the cacophony of ungodly screams and sounds that stood the hair on the back of her neck. She landed with a thud, the air knocked from her lungs. She fought to catch her breath, stretching her head back, and gasping.

She saw the space above her; the ceiling shined like copper. Undulating colors slowly formed an image...

A woman wearing a long dress sat beside a bed where a little girl lay. As she stroked the child's thrashing head, Karen sensed death. The woman neither wavered in her comforting touch, nor tired from her faithful mission. Karen reached out to the vision that dissolved before her eyes.

The sounds of pain grew stronger, and a soldier staggered into view, his fist tearing into his chest as if he could massage his heart back to life. She gasped as another uniformed hero came running, then knelt beside his fallen comrade, and the men held tight to each other until death claimed its victim.

An unbearable and all-consuming pain filled the chamber, the vision changed again. Looking away was impossible as more faces drifted across the canvas on the cavern wall. An old man appeared. He was walking a bride on his arm, and then, he handed her over to her groom who he had known to be a murderer. Karen saw the old man fighting his tears as she felt his anguish.

She closed her eyes, momentarily, to keep from taking another look. Flames crawled across an ancient city. The emperor fiddled while his people burned. She heard every scream and saw every melting body; the husbands frantically searching for wives, and mothers agonizing in cries for their lost children.

As one scene dissolved before her, another appeared. She saw a great plain littered with hundreds of animal carcasses.

The face of an American Indian woman stared back at her. Karen watched the woman raise her arms as she began to trill, the sharp pitch of her sound sending Karen's mind into sorrow that she thought would break her heart. Karen blinked to the vision, and suddenly realized that the things floating around the woman's head were her dismembered hands.

"Stop this hellish torment!" Karen screamed.

The sight of thousands of emaciated men marching behind barbed wire, their striped pajamas caked with dirt and stained with blood, as hollowed eyes stared out to her from gaunt faces of great deprivation, but not resignation.

Karen prayed for relief--a moment's reprieve from the nightmares--and then, she saw the familiar figure. "Mignon," she gasped, moving closer to the wall. The black woman looked like Mignon, but she was much too young, struggling to stand, and appearing to be pregnant. Karen flinched at the repeated sound of a whip, and felt her stomach heave as the deep-cut ruts in the woman's back bled and ran down her dress.

"Why?" Karen shouted.

Her parent's head-on automobile crash flashed across the wall. The driver's face surfaced, his light forming silent words apologizing for the unpardonable thing he'd done. He had been driving drunk.

"Karen," a tender, gentle voice called out to her.

Her tear-ladden eyes looked up as a fiery light obliterated the glow in her palm.

"Was it just hours ago that you held me in your hands?"

"Grace?" Karen said in disbelief. Her knees buckled. "Dear Lord, help me," she begged her Creator.

"Karen," The voice again called; soft and comforting, as her mother's voice had always been. A pain more intense than she had ever felt flooded her heart. "Mother? ... Grace?" She pressed the palms of her hands against her eyes fighting to resist that which had so much control over her.

"Stop the nightmares! Dundury *is* evil--all consuming and hellish!"

"Evil--only in Dundury, Karen?" the voice laughed a grotesque sound. "That is not so," the taunting voice insisted. "You have been honored with the visions of the humidor. You have seen the evil that has crossed every generation, every human endeavor."

A slow dawning crept into Karen's soul. *Is this what Sherman saw? Is this what made him an instrument of evil?* She shuddered. "Evil yes, but, these visions are filled with something else," she said, suddenly resigned in the truth that would not be silenced.

The soft response was, "Yes," drowned out in the torrent of water that flooded the room and dragged Karen down to the floor.

"Grace! Don't leave me," she cried out as her face surfaced the water. "Grace!" Karen screamed. "Oh, Mother! Please help me!"

Hell mocked her, freezing her limbs so that she couldn't move in the deluge of water that covered her, twisting her round in its current of wrath. Then, as quickly as it had cascaded over her, it receded and the ground writhed beneath her.

"Kittendorf? Where are you," she begged, trying to stand in the cavernous pit.

"He has been washed away. His thoughts of valor were laughable,"

"Who are you? she demanded.

"I am time immortal. I scoff at the plight you find so abhorrent. I am the mover of all things and, you, are my puppet."

"Never!"

"Do not dare to challenge me, girl. I will break you, as I have all the others."

"Never," Karen wailed before falling to the floor.

Ava Lindsey Chambers

Chapter 14

"We've got to do something," Bob said, grabbing Davis by his hair and yanking him to his feet. "She's down there!"

"Down *where?*" Lisa asked, her eyes widening as she followed his pointing finger.

"Under the earth. Something dragged her down there-- from where there's no return. The stump is the doorway to--" Bob winced. "Listen to those screams!"

"No, it's coming from somewhere else. We heard those sounds before she disappeared."

Bob stepped closer to Davis until they were nose to nose. "You sat by this stump and it made you sick," Bob said, growing impatient. "But, it took Karen."

A scream came from the orifice-- Karen's scream.

"Oh, God! Please help her! Help me." Bob said, falling to his knees, his fingers frantically digging into the loose dirt. Suddenly, he felt the fine smooth wood of the humidor. Fighting tears, he sat back trying to remember what he was taught-- what he should do. "It's the humidor."

"Buried in peace, yet doomed to turmoil. Find what you seek, look deep, look deep," Davis said in a low haunting voice.

Red-eyed and frightened, Bob looked from Davis to Lisa. "I love her. I didn't fully realize it before--but, I do. I love her."

"Great," Davis said, kneeling down beside Bob. "You think you can save her?"

Bob stared into his friend's eyes. "You know more than I do, Davis. You lived in Dundury, plus you researched all this," he said, then turned to Lisa. "What about all those papers the children wrote in your class. There must have been something--anything!"

"No, not about this," Lisa said. "I tried to get Mignon to tell me things, but she only offered silly rhymes and demented stories."

"There's the book," Davis said, standing. "It looked blank to us, but Karen saw something."

"And the dust, Father said something about the dust." Bob rubbed his head, trying to remember. "Karen mentioned some woman named Ruth who knew secrets about our family. She said Ruth worked for you."

"So?" Davis stared back at Bob.

"Kittendorf is gone. Karen is gone. No matter what you say, those screams are coming up from beneath the stump. Help me!"

"You and Karen put the potions together," Davis said. "What were you expecting?"

"At the time, I was keeping them from Father." Bob shouted and began to pace. "There are the little ones and us and... Karen is not--"

"Yes," Davis interrupted. "What do you know?"

"The Lucifer's were important," Bob said. "But, I can't remember."

"The Lucifer's were just a joke," Davis said, smirking.

Bob punched him.

"Stop it!" Lisa shouted at the two of them. "What are you going to do, beat it out of him? He's sick and he's trying."

"He's been a fraud all his life. He's not sick, just manipulative." Bob fisted his hands. "You better tell me."

"Nooooo." The sound, hollow and deep, drew their attention.

"I'm going to find a way down there," Bob said and started digging again.

Lisa and Davis just stood there watching Bob. Huge clumps of dirt flew through the air. Like a badger, Bob dug faster and faster. Suddenly, he broke through to something. The humidor. He tried to pry it loose.

"No, don't open it!" Lisa rushed to Bob; something flung her backward. Davis stood holding onto her shirt, an odd grin possessing his lips. Then, he vanished leaving her rooted to the spot.

Bob's head and neck, then his torso descended into the stump. He found himself sliding down a tunnel.

"Well, well, well," a voice said through an evil laugh. "Two for the price of one."

"Who are you?"

"An old friend of the family."

Bob squinted in the near darkness. *I'm here, under the world. God help me.*

Something billowed in front of him. It seemed like a robe. Black and purple, it shimmered, it's odd brilliance disguising a body. Fingers were hidden beneath the long full sleeves, while feet dangled lifeless from the hem.

Bob began to see through the maze of flowing fabric as it rose above him. "How'd you get up there?"

"An old wizard's trick. I have been an exceptional and masterful wizard of fine repute for several centuries."

"What the hell are you talking about?"

"*Hell*, now, that is the key word. It means you and your

Karen are mine now, and I have great plans for us."

"Who are you?"

"Come now, Bob, you must remember."

The sound of Karen's voice came softly, weakly, from a distance.

"Karen?" Bob called out to her. Sound flooded the chamber and Bob covered his ears. "Stop it! There's no need to torture us." The roar increased.

"Torture? What a splendid idea."

"Bob," Karen called out.

"I'm here!"

"Exactly where is *here*?" she said.

"Inside the earth, my dear, to be precise." Laughter overcame the noise. "You mortals are a stupid race. None of you has figured it out yet." Another cackle followed the words as the roaring noise ceased. "Centuries ago, I tried to help. I was fine tuning my craft then. I tried to put ideas in the minds of men. I hoped for helpers, followers. Great leaders emerged, but the rest of your backward race called them crazy."

Karen appeared in the light of the robe. She tried to stand up. "The earth has an inside."

"It's hollow, like a big round candy mountain. And, oh, those who inhabit our space will delight you, indeed."

"Don't listen, Karen," Bob urged her. "You don't believe in magic. Facts-- remember? That's your strength."

"But, my hand. Look at it," she said, extending it to him. "It's glowing."

"You've received some of the power," the voice said. "I don't know how, but you have. You, belong here--with me."

Karen looked more afraid than any human Bob had ever seen. "Bob, am I small? Did that thing do something to me? I feel so very odd."

He rushed to her side. "No, Karen. You can't be made small. Remember, it's all just nonsense."

"But, the book? And, Mignon? She had magic. I didn't

believe at first," she said turning to search her surroundings.

The tormentor's voice squealed, "You know where you are, Karen. Inside the earth, where the world began. The super-race was formed here. It's the beginning of all things. Think about the trees. The roots tunnel down for food, down to the source of all life."

"They also grow up to the light. Trees give us the very air we depend on." Bob's voice was stressed.

"Yes, but the source of all strength comes from here, deep in the earth. The nourishment, the stability, everything comes from us." A laugh, loud and hurtful, erupted. "And, of course, you bury your dead. All the tears fall back into the hole, back to us."

"Who are you?" Karen demanded, rubbing her temples. "Why did you bring me here?"

"You sealed your own fate. You involved yourself in something that was best left alone."

"Lisa and Davis knew Grace, too. And, what about all the other houses in town? None of it makes any sense!"

"It will, my dear. It will."

Bob glanced up at the apparition, suddenly recognizing the creature. "You can't tell. It will mean your end."

"I have survived for centuries. I am the one who sent explorers to go to the polar ice caps in the 1800's. They found an opening to the inner world. They were ridiculed, and so, they gave up. It was a loss, they were so close to getting in." Floating higher and higher the voice began to sound familiar, even to Karen.

Inching closer to Bob, she whispered, "Why would it want humans to find a way in here? I thought we were stupid," she said.

"Stupid, indeed, but necessary. The two worlds were created to be separate. Our people are very advanced. We knew the human race would never understand us. Yet, there were always some of us who thought they could change the plan that was put forth since the beginning.

"So, your people need our people," Karen said.

"Well, not exactly. We found the little people didn't provide enough--" The apparition, for a moment, seemed at a loss. "Amusement, you might say. Then they found a way to escape us, popping out in the land that you call Ireland."

"They created the legends of leprechauns and fairies," Karen said.

"Yes, fairies, leprechauns and the sort were seen by humans. Stupid little beasts thought they had been enslaved. They didn't understand that we created them. Their leaders were sure that life on the outside would be better."

"Tell her how they got out," Bob said.

"You know so much, Bob, you tell her."

"The cracks in the earth were brought about by the magic of the under-lords. Every hardship a human suffers has been caused by them. The bastards create and thrive on discord. Human trials are so much richer than any other.

"But," Karen began. "How do the little ones get out?"

"The little people surface when the world is asunder," Bob said. "In America it happened during the Civil War. It was brother against brother, son against father, the worst time in our history."

The vile, floating entity clapped it's hands. "Yes, delightful time, that was."

"The little people came out because the lords were distracted," Karen said, trying to understand the mystery.

"Exactly! When the under-lords are wreaking havoc on humans, they tend to focus less on the little ones," Bob said. "That's when they're able to escape."

"And Grace being outside meant that some evil had occurred which allowed her escape."

"Escape," the voice bellowed. "That's what started it all, ideas of freedom. How ridiculous for creatures that exist because we will them to be so."

"Freedom is the desire of all living things, most especially humans," Karen said, staring at Bob who refused to return her look.

"You are a subspecies. To me, you are like a mosquito that I absently swat away," the voice thundered."

"Then, why am I here? Why am I so valuable?" Karen challenged.

"You know something that he can never understand," Bob said. "What have you learned?"

"I've seen things here," Karen said, holding the look in Bob's eyes. "Humans exist because they can love. I've been told that since I came to Dundury." She couldn't take her eyes from his. "But, there's something else..."

"The under people lost the capacity for love a long time ago. They tried to create a world of order and higher thinking. Instead, they labored with Lucifer to intensify evil."

"Oh, my, aren't we proper. Love is the savior of the world," the mocking voice rang out in rage.

"Why did Mignon bury the little people in a humidor, Bob?" Karen asked.

"It looks the most like this place, I suppose. It gave them a sense of coming home, of being safe."

The floating creature sank to the floor in front of them. "Sentimental fools! Isn't that stupid! The little love's in a tobacco box. Ha! That just gave us one more idea. Smoke and flames destroy mankind from the inside out!"

"Bob, I think I know how to get out of here."

"There is no *out*," the voice bellowed.

"I think Davis wanted me to love him," Karen said, looking close at the apparition, trying to find a face. "Look in my eyes, Davis. I know it's you in that stupid robe. You aren't evil."

Bob pulled her back. "That thing can't be Davis. I left him with Lisa."

Karen reached up and ripped the cape off the apparition.

"It is Davis. Don't you see, it all fits. He wants help and your family, his family, its all he has to hope for."

"No!" Bob screamed. "We've got to get out of here before we're consumed."

"Bob, we can save him or doom him. It's our choice. Even that little mosquito he talked about carries a deadly virus."

"We can't save anything here," Bob warned. "The under lords are too powerful."

Karen shook her head refusing to accept what he was saying.

Bob reached out to her. "All we can do is close them off from our world."

"You think I can't hear your words! That I don't know your thoughts!" The voice boomed and vibrated in their heads.

"As can I," a tender voice echoed.

With whirling thunder, the thing turned to face his age-old enemy. "You!" He recoiled. "It's not possible!"

"Run, Karen," Bob screamed, pushing her toward the opening in the wall. "We can make it now!"

"I can't see!"

"Hold out your hand."

"Bob! We have to help! We--" A crushing noise filled the chamber choking off her words in the doom-filled space. Sounds of battle, curses, shrieks, and clanging noises followed their flight.

Chapter
15

"Will you please stop pushing me!"

"I didn't touch you. I can barely keep up. How can you move so fast?"

"I don't know. I thought something was helping me or pushing me," Karen said. "I just know we've got to get out."

"Good, you keep going! I'm going back."

"You can't!" she screamed.

Bob struggled to catch his breath. "That voice was Bertha's. She's come to help us. I won't let anything happen to her," he said.

Karen turned around to him. "I've heard and seen some damn strange things since I've been in Dundury. I even talked to Grace! But none of it's real, Bob," she said. "Bertha is in Marietta, taking care of your magazine."

"It's her, she's here," Bob insisted.

"You want her to be here."

He hung his head and took a moment to collect himself. "This is all part of the final battle. I never knew how it would happen. I thought, perhaps, Father, but," he paused, "I was wrong."

"I don't understand!"

"The battle has been set for ages. Now its come and Bertha is all we have on our side."

"I heard about the two little girls watching when your grandparents had their trouble." Her hand glowed even brighter as she lifted it to his face. "Who were those little girls?"

"Mignon and Bertha. They're sisters," he said, softly.

"That's what I mean. Bob, it's not possible. They're not that old."

"They are, Karen. It's part of the magic. Their people consisted of many races. They lived a long, long time."

"In Dundury?"

"Mostly, I think. I guess the first little ones appeared during the Trail of Tears. Mignon and Bertha's parents discovered them, guarded then, loved them and buried them."

"In a humidor?"

"Yes."

An eerie moan filled the cavern.

"Come on," Bob whispered.

"Are we going forward or backwards?"

"I've got to help Bertha. She's all we have on our side."

"Because Mignon is gone," Karen said.

"Yes," he said, heavily. "She always knew that fire would claim her."

"That's why she was so afraid of the Lucifer's."

"She knew her end meant that the final battle would begin."

Karen shook her head in disbelief. "There were signs?"

"Yes," Bob said.

"Signs that were visible to us?"

"Who do you mean *us*?" Bob asked.

"The human race, dummy!"

"It was Bertha's idea to call you. She must have known."

In the lightning flash of a moment, the world that held them shook. Mud and debris rained down on them as a crack split the earth, belching up its unholy incense.

"Something wants me down here," Karen yelled. The scar on her hand pulsated, as if warning her.

Bob's knees buckled. "Something's on top of me. Karen, are you there?" An awful silence consumed their surroundings. "Here for a reason," Bob said to himself.

Karen screamed, grabbing at the dirt that fell on top of her. "Bob-- I'm falling!"

"Can you hear it?"

"I don't hear anything," she yelled back.

"Whatever was here is gone. Bertha is gone."

The light in Karen's hand slowly dimmed. "We've got to find a way to get out of here before it comes back."

Bob clawed at the dirt that encased Karen.

"We'll get out and destroy this place," she said, wiggling and squirming to loosen herself from the dirt that nearly entombed her. "We can get some of the machines at Davis' house. We'll dig this place out!"

Bob shook his head. "No. This world will annihilate all that mankind has ever known."

"We *can* stop it," she insisted. "You can't give up. What about the Kittendorf bloodline? What about your training?"

"Karen, it's over. Evil has won."

"I won't believe that!" she said, crawling closer to him. "Evil can't win."

"It's too late," he said. "Bertha and Mignon are gone. We're lost without them."

"So, what do you suggest we do?"

"Pray, Karen. Pray for your soul."

Karen fought the urge to slap him. "*Pray?* That's all you have to offer? I've prayed my whole life, and where has it gotten me-- caught in the pit of hell, that's where."

"Everyone comes to prayer sooner or later. Maybe it's at the point of death or of great suffering, but it comes to us all."

"That's it, then?" Karen said.

"I don't know what else to say," he confessed in the futility of what seemed his inevitable fate.

A voice called out his name. It was Bertha's voice. "Bob, it is time."

"Go ahead, Karen, follow your feelings. I'm staying here," he said.

"You're supposed to stay here--and die?"

"Don't you hear Bertha calling me?" Bob said.

"Your imagining things. Now *dig!*"

"Tell her, Bob." Bertha's voice encouraged. "Remember the door."

He fell back down onto the mound of dirt; his head fell forward into his hands. "A door?"

"What door?"

"The door to the heart," he said, pulling himself up and staggering toward her voice. "I need you, Karen."

The earth trembled beneath and above him as each falling rock belched its landing in the murky mud below. "Bertha, you taught me all I know and loved me as a mother." Screams answered his pleas. "I call upon all of Heaven's power and you, Lord, please hear me."

"I hear you," Evil answered.

Karen stood speechless, her eyes wide like a deer in the headlights of an oncoming car. Streaks of green and purple zigged and zagged across the cavern walls. Reason fought for control of her mind. Her eyes widened, then squinted trying to see something, *anything*. Shrieks and screams overtook the silence, chilling her blood. She began to run, cautiously at first, feeling the firmness of the earth and then, it's murky mush pulling her down like quicksand. Suddenly, she smacked headlong into a wall, knocking her to the ground as familiar voices grew louder.

"It is you," Bob said, focusing on the figure materializing before him and the face illumined with evil.

"Yes, it's me.," Davis said. "My time has finally come. You hoped I was gone-- or, perhaps, dead?"

"I hoped you were well."

"Liar!"

"I prayed that none of this was real."

"You *prayed?* Which of us was more tortured," he asked through a contemptuous laugh. "Kittendorf thought he could change our destiny."

"He meant well," Bob said.

Davis paced around him. "Karen brought me such hope. I couldn't believe she fit into the gown. How beautiful she was!"

"How many women were there before Karen?"

"It took nearly all of the last ten years to search for my special woman. At first, couples on their honeymoon came to Dundury," Davis giggled. "The Inn provided a lovely bed and, of course, breakfast."

"What did you do to them," Bob asked, his face a blank mask.

"I merely invited the ladies to stay and join our *club*. Some were truly beautiful. I gave each and every one the opportunity to try on the lovely period clothes, join the banquets, and become revered in Dundury. They needed to feel better about themselves."

"And you convinced these brides to stay in Dundury."

"They adored me. I even convinced one to leave her groom."

"What did you do with *him?*"

"We got him drunk...helped him drown all of his pitiful sorrows," Davis laughed. Unfortunately, he had an automobile accident--crashed head on into a couple, just outside of Marietta."

Bob felt his heartbeats thundering. "Karen's family?"

"Now, do you really think I have that much power, dear cousin?" His smirk said so many things.

Bob refused to answer.

"Well, I do! I *learned* the secrets of Dundury," he said, leaning into Bob's face with a sneer that made Bob's skin crawl.

"Really?" Bob increased the distance between them. "And, your powers grew?"

Davis gave him a slow nod. "Every time I worked my magic, the suffering grew worse--the sores, the meltdown, you know the drill. I almost gave in," he said, clapping his hands with glee, advancing on Bob. "I did perfect one thing." He grabbed Bob's shoulders and spun him around. "I can contain a person's essence!"

Bob restrained the urge to punch Davis square in the nose.

"I can contain a person's essence--their soul, their power, their being!"

"How?"

"Lisa started it, actually; when she moved back into her grandmother's house. I thought she knew something..." Davis paused.

"But?"

A smirk slowly formed; his timing was perfection. "From the school children. Their stories were so informative. No one had bothered to properly educate the children in what they could and couldn't tell," he said, hushing his lips with a finger, then whispered. "We're not supposed to tell, are we? Play dumb, act stupid, that's how Dundury has saved its secrets."

"Did you know that one of the little people gave up her essence for your grandmother?" Davis said, his breath fouling the air between them. "How does that make you feel? Important?"

"No, Davis, it makes me sad."

Davis laughed. "Her essence was in a little person.

Someone died so that your grandmother could live--even after she had caused such desolation."

"She tried to guard the truth, to protect millions."

"Oh, and my grandfather didn't?"

"You know he didn't."

"All the Kittendorf's thought he was dead. But I'll tell you the truth--" Davis said, his nose nearly touching Bob's. "He gave his essence to me." He glared deep into Bob's eyes, trying to penetrate his mind. "I have his knowledge, his power, and all that he learned from outer earth, as well as inner earth. I am the strongest lord who ever came to be!"

Bob grabbed hold of Davis, his fingers brushing against something shimmering in Davis' hand. Bertha moaned.

"A little ball," Davis said, holding the orb in his extended hand so that Bob could see the masterdom he had achieved.

Bob's breathing accelerated.

"Look closer," Davis shouted. "Should I shake her? She's in here, you know. Do you hear her," he screamed, reaching into the pocket inside his robe. "Recognize these?"

Bob nodded. "Lucifer's."

Davis loomed over Bob, his height increasing moment by moment. "You think you've known me all these years," he screamed, his voice thundering in the cavernous abyss. "I transcend time. I followed you, and abandoned you, and now I am back for you."

Bob swallowed hard. "Where is Kittendorf?"

"The evil one has him. Don't you feel sorry now, after you misjudged him," he sneered. "When all the time it was *me*." Laughter bellowed out of Davis' while he rolled the little ball in the palms of his hands.

"Bob," Bertha's voice was barely audible.

"Let her out!" Bob demanded.

"Why? She's small enough to fit into my hand? Someone is finally made small. Funny, isn't it?"

"Let her go!"

"Why should I? So she can warn the rest of her kind. This isn't really her, you know. It's her essence. Can you fathom that, Bob?"

"I was taught-- just like you," Bob said, fighting the urge to grab Davis around his neck and squeeze the life out of him. "Does it give you joy to make her cry,"

"Yes, it does," Davis said, throwing the ball up against the ceiling. "Now her misery is added to all the other pictures within the humidor." He towered over Bob, then leaned down to him. "Poor, Bob, should I add you, or your beautiful Karen next?"

Chapter 16

Lisa sat alone. Somewhere buried within her memory there had to be an answer, but now even the questions seemed as vaporous clouds. "Davis? Where are you?" The air was still and, then, she realized the world had returned to normal. Hot winds no longer blew and the sky broke into a beautiful dawn in usual Georgia brilliance. *Is it finished*, she wondered and, in response, a calico cat appeared and sat down beside her.

Each stroke against its fur brought comfort to Lisa. She leaned back against the stump. "You're a pretty girl, aren't you?" The cat's face couldn't have been more perfect if an artist had drawn it. Black ears tipped with ochre and a clump of white for a nose gave way to auburn cheeks. "Isn't it a beautiful day?"

Lisa yawned then closed her eyes. The purring cat snuggled in her lap. *Forget, forget, forget* pounded her brain with each vibration. Deeper and deeper Lisa slipped into the realm halfway between wakefulness and slumber. Dreams of hot summer days and lemonade and soft Southern voices brought comfort and sleep. Memories of family and friends sparked a moment in time that sought its escape.

"Davis," she heard herself say. "Something's here to..." Her eyelids closed tightly as her memory fought to control the weavings of her mind. Light, airy wisps floated in her dream. The cat stood on Lisa's lap, circled three times, and situated herself in a tight ball. Louder it purred, digging claws through the fabric of her slacks and into the supple skin of Lisa's thighs.

Her eyes flew open. "Ouch! You're the one taking my strength, my will. Get off me!" She whacked the cat's behind; it sailed into the air. It had the audacity to return and sit within inches of her, staring into her eyes.

She felt the stump vibrating behind her. "Davis--are you in there, too?" she said, kneeling and staring down into the orifice. She grabbed at the dirt. "It stopped." She shook the stump, then pushed her hands into the cool powder inside it, trying to remember.

The cat ventured closer.

"Stay where you are. Cats aren't allowed in Dundury." The animal purred its response. "Stop that! I've got to help my friends." A sudden feeling of helplessness forced her tears. "Mignon! She'll help me." With one last glance at the stump, she stood up and ran into the woods. She dared not look behind her, lest that damned cat would be encouraged to follow.

Hunger rumbled in Lisa's stomach as the fingers of morning caressed her soul. *Nothing could be as beautiful as this place,* she told herself. As she cleared the woods, the charred remains of Mignon's home triggered snippets of her memory. Fire and pain as fresh as yesterday had almost been obliterated. *Why,* resounded in her brain.

"Mignon?" Her legs carried her closer to the house. Black

soot and smoldering embers in the chimney were all that remained. Lisa searched for the body. "Oh, my poor Mignon."

A meow answered and Lisa ran to her car.

Mignon's package lay on the backseat floorboard. She opened the back car door, reached in and grabbed the package. She ran around the trunk, to the driver's door, stumbled, then looked down. "The book," she whispered, wiping the tears from her face. "It's the *whole* book."

She bent over and picked it up and a gust of wind lifted the cover and blew open the pages. Drawings, vile and beautiful, gave way to the other realm. Bloody stumps of men and weeping women were covered by gossamer wings. *Was this a war of the angels, a war of the past, or of the future?* Her eyes closed in prayer.

The cat sneaked closer.

"The rhyme," Lisa muttered, frantically turning the pages. The book grew heavy; its words appearing foreign. "It's gibberish," she said, dropping to her knees in prayer. "God is good, God is great..." A rumble of thunder challenged her words. "I will lift up mine eyes to the Lord..." Again, a thundercrack interrupted her, as if angered by her attempt. "I will seek the Lord, *always*..."

The vision of a deep and turbulent river filled her mind. Raging rapids tossed, then sucked Bob below the surface; he was drowning in the depths and there was no way to reach him. The book levitated out of her hands. Water dripped from it's spine.

"No! Dear God, no!" she begged her Creator. The book danced before her, as if urging her to take it and open it again. She reached for it, but the book only tempted her, gliding backwards, just beyond her reach. "Well, fine! Take me to your master."

Fluttering like a butterfly, the book continued its flight. She followed after it with Mignon's package still tucked under her arm. The cat darted between her feet, sometimes holding her back, sometimes pushing her forward. She stopped and looked up to see--not the book--but Davis standing before her.

"You're all right, then," she said.

"Yes." The beautiful smile she had loved ignited his face. His cream colored suit, decked with his gold watch chain, and his cigar in hand told her he'd been safe. "Lisa, what have you been doing?" he asked, his voice smooth and seductive.

"Sleeping, I think. There was a cat, you see. It came back and purred, then lay in my lap."

"Nothing else? You did nothing else?"

"I went to Mignon's, but--" her gaze fell from his. "You know she's gone."

"Yes, then what did you do?"

"I saw the book, but it seems to be gone now, too."

"You did something else. I heard you." Anger replaced the sultry sound of his voice.

"No, Davis."

"Then who did I hear praying?" The rumble that she thought was thunder spewed from his voice.

"Well, yes, I guess I did pray some."

His eyes bored deep into hers. "Why did you pray?"

Her shoulders slumped, her knees buckled to the hard ground as she fell to her knees. "Why pray? We pray because-- because it's all we have, Davis."

"Who is *we*?" With the grace of a leopard he moved over her. "Tell me, Lisa. Exactly what do you know?" His hand wrapped tightly around her neck. She cried. "And why would *you* pray?"

"Stop it, you're hurting me!" She reached for his hand. "I was taught to pray, it strengthens the soul."

Disgust curled his lip and he pushed her, she landed on her back. "Either you are very very stupid, or very, very enlightened. I can't decide which."

"You don't believe in the power of God?"

"I believe stronger than anyone you'll ever know, my

dear. I have waged war against that so-called divine spirit for generations," he said, snarling his contempt.

Her eyes went wide as she ventured a step closer to him. "Your face-- the sores are coming back."

"It's the air," he whined. "And your prayers."

She glanced beyond him and saw it--the cat had led her back to the stump. "You know how to save Karen and Bob."

His laugh shook the trees, heaving up moans under the very dirt on which they stood. "Save them? They're trapped by their own frailties. Bob needs Karen to love him, and Karen has lost her faith. Neither will find what they desperately need to survive."

The calico cat brushed her ankles. "We must help them," she said, glancing down to the cat. "This animal seems to take my will."

"Yes, a particularly useful contribution from the little people," he said as an intense heat began to radiate from him. "Forget the cat, come with me."

"Are we going to help Bob and Karen?"

"Of course, my dear," he said, his voice as smooth as the wolf in grandma's bed. "We'll help them into eternity."

Lisa followed, seeing the sores multiplying on his neck. *Is he really so evil?* A prayer escaped her.

He yanked her hand

"Where's Mignon's book?" she said, trying to keep pace with him.

"The book is useless now."

She stumbled. "Where are we going?"

"To my house. I need a few things."

Tears spilled down her face. She had loved him once, even planned a life with him. How blind she had been. A thump on her back made her jump and she turned, barely able to glance behind her. The book hovered and darkness closed in around her.

Awareness returned and they were walking up a long graveled drive that approached a Georgian plantation. *Is this his home?*

He stretched out his arm in grandiose delight. "My palace awaits," he said, dragging her up the steps and across the threshold.

"You never told me about this place," she said, struggling to keep up with him. "And, your servants?"

"There is no one here, my dear," he said, turning around to her inside, at the foot of the spiral staircase. "Only we two." He started up the stairs two by two, impatient with her slow compliance, then dragged her down the long hall, and burst open the bedroom doors.

Lisa shuddered. "No! I won't," she screamed, unable to move, the package still tucked under her arm.

His laughter bounced off the rafters until silence surrounded them. He caressed her cheek, then kissed her passionately. "I don't want your body," he said, the pupils of his eyes turning a coal black. "I want your soul."

She couldn't scream, nor breathe through the vice-grip his arms held around her. A knock at the front door sent him running to the window.

"Ignore it," he ordered, returning to her. "Look here," he said, pulling her across the polished wood floor to his marble-topped dresser. "My collection of orbs." Tapered fingers pointed to the bright spheres filled with shimmering colors. "I collected them from the four corners of the world. Today, I shall make my own spheres of--" He went to the three-legged mahogany table and the package she'd carried since finding it in her car.

"I just had that. It's--"

He sauntered back to her, rubbing his chin, and smiling. "Let's see, you were to mail it to Karen," he said in a whisper, wrapping his arms around her and bringing her close in an embrace. "But, you see, my dear, I need it. Karen wouldn't know how to use these potions."

Lisa surveyed the room for a way to escape; there was none except for the door. More knocks, sounding louder and more persistent, continued. "Shouldn't we answer the door?"

"Sit down." He pointed to the bed. "If I can perform the magic while earthbound, I will rule all. You're my first try."

Lisa began to tremble, too frightened to speak. *First try-- at what?*

"It's easy when I'm down under. But here above, there are so many challenges." He searched the bottles, occasionally looking up at her, and then made his selections.

"I won't be a part of your madness. Karen got away, so will I."

He reached into the box and pulled the veil; in that instant he let out a bloodcurdling scream. With the mere touch of it, his fingers began to boil. "Damn you, Mignon!" He lowered his chin and his eyes fired the hate he had for Lisa. "And you, what have you done?"

"I didn't do anything! I packed the box just as I was told." Her eyes moved beyond Davis and settled on the window. *It's the book.*

Davis dropped to his knees, moaning and holding out his hands, the flesh bubbling up in a festering ooze. "Mend, fingers." He concentrated, oblivious to everything else as he willed his flesh to heal. "Now, we proceed. Get rid of that damned veil and pull out the bottles."

She set each bottle on the bedside table; some held powder, some liquid. "What is all this?"

"It's the magic that will give me power over all the earth. And now, thanks to Karen and Bob, I have not only the ingredients, but also the recipe."

"Recipe?"

"Of course, Mignon only knew a piece of the formula. The rest is the little rhyme."

"What rhyme?"

"It was the *sons to fathers* part that threw me. I thought Bob, of the Kittendorf bloodline, would have to be offered up. Fortunately, my grandfather discovered secrets, too," he said, then clapped his hands together like a happy child. "And now, I have all of the proportions. The magic of the ages, the serums of Succubus."

"And they are?"

"Twice four to eight." He sat on the edge of the bed. "You will put out two rows of the potions. They must be mixed exactly."

"What do I mix them with?"

"You fool! There's a spoon in the box."

A wooden spoon with strange markings inscribed on the handle lay on the bottom of the box. "I see it."

"Good, put a spoonful of each powder on the table. Make two rows and take care not to mix them."

"What about the liquid?"

He fisted the headboard of the bed. "Did I tell you to touch that? It must be exact!" He bolted off the bed and started pacing and muttering. "Incompetent human subspecies."

"Now what?"

"When you pour the liquid it will harden. I have two bowls. Measure equal amounts of each liquid."

"But then it will mix. Isn't that wrong?"

His brow lifted in contempt for her obvious stupidity. "It must not mix until it has made four-- do you understand, *four!*"

"Then you need more bowls. This makes no sense." He fisted the headboard again. "I can't have forgotten anything. I've roamed for generations collecting."

"Maybe you should drink it."

"No, stupid woman! It makes the glass orbs." He picked up a ball. "See, we will make *this*."

"Why?"

"I told you why! These little baubles hold the essence of great leaders," he said, picking up one that glowed with a horrible blackness. "Hitler," he said, holding it out to her. "This one is the most ancient. See the orange flame. Lucifer, as some called him. Now that I have them, I have their power."

"Power to do what?"

"To live in both worlds, to come and go as I please. Respect from each realm, that is what I seek."

Lisa shuddered and dumped an extra half spoonful of powder into one of the piles. Thankfully, Davis didn't seem to notice.

"Now, I rake them together." He reached into his breast pocket and removed a tiny brush. "Isn't it magnificent? Not one magic word is necessary." The beautiful smile she remembered graced his face. "My dear, come closer."

A knock sounded at the window. "Davis, look! It's the book--it's hovering outside!" When he turned, she threw one of the balls at the window and ran for the door. The veil twisted around her legs as she made her escape.

Ava Lindsey Chambers

Chapter 17

Karen sat up trying to remember where she was. Slime and muck covered her. The longing for a shower and a toothbrush had its own special torment. she licked the inside of her mouth. "Bob? Bertha?" She stood up, stretched and suddenly gasped in pain as both knees popped. Shadows crept along the chamber walls, sometimes glowing, always disturbing. "Bob, I've figured it out. The humidor keeps the essence Davis talked about. Bob, are you still here?" She took a step backwards.

She glanced down at her palm, relieved that the scar hadn't changed. Another step in an unidentifiable direction fixed her resolve to stop worrying and take control of whatever fate held in store for her. "Bob, answer me!"

A moan, weak and sounding far away, echoed softly. "We're inside the humidor, that's why there's the strange light. We've got to push up and out, I think," Karen said, as she punched the darkness above her head. She felt nothing. Her feet were sinking. "Bob, it's getting wet again."

"I can't breathe," he said breathlessly.

"We're gonna make it, Bob." *I refuse to let fear get in my head. I have reasons to live.*

"Karen, he killed Bertha-- my only friend."

"I don't think she's really gone," Karen said, biting her lower lip. "And, you've got me." Her foot slipped into a hole that sucked her down. *Stay still*, she thought. Calm came from exhaustion.

"Something is on my head--it's pushing me down. I won't be able to breathe much longer."

"Put up your hand. Do you feel anything?"

"I'm in some sort of air pocket. If I move I'm afraid of a cave in."

"Well, try!"

Something grabbed Karen's ankle. "Bob! It's me on top of you. Hold on, pull up and you'll be free."

"No, you'll sink too."

"I won't. Remember, I have some sort of power," Karen said, shaking her head and trying to believe her own words. "Pull, Bob, and I'll pull too. We'll go up. I just know it."

Fear was not going to be her master. Slowly and with focused attention, she pulled each foot free. "I'm out, Bob. Can you hear me?" One of Bob's hands was wrapped around her ankle. "Think of all the good in the world. Come with me."

Out from the muck popped his face, his lips agape as he frantically pulled in air. "We're free," he said, once his breathing had stabilized.

"Not exactly," Karen laughed. "But we're together. I know what Mignon meant now. The world is about to change."

"It's Davis, you know. He's the key," he said, pulling himself up and out of the murky mush. "You think we're in the humidor--so how do we get out?"

"We push up?"

Bob rubbed his eyes. "I think I've lost Bertha. Davis took her," he whispered. "She's part of the sadness now."

"She'll be remembered the way we choose to. Her life and her will were of great value." Karen reached out to him and felt a stir inside her heart. "Hold my hand, Bob. Let's crawl up."

"There's nothing to hold on to."

"Hold to me. We go together. Concentrate on moving up to the light. Think of truth, and goodness. You told me to believe once. Now it's your turn to have faith."

"I was trained to recognize truth, but that was a long time ago," he said, shaking his head. "I thought my father was evil. I didn't believe the things Bertha told me."

"Believe now. Something brought us down here and that means we *can* get out."

"The world is doomed to fail. Humans are too weak and too sin filled."

Karen fought the urge to kick him. "Stop it! The wrong thought will doom us."

"What?" His voice sounded odd, as if some other voice were speaking.

"Remember, the trees grow up to the light."

"Right, but the roots are in the earth."

"Well, maybe part of us hails from here, but we live outside. We think and feel the things that matter. That's why we'll make it."

"The little people didn't make it. They fought for truth and they're still bound here."

"Don't be negative, Bob. It'll make us fail. Besides there are little ones out there, too. Think of Grace." Karen stretched her arm as far above her head as she could; she felt a ledge. Slowly and steadily, she hoisted herself up.

"Grace is gone."

At his words, Karen slipped downward. "Stop it! There are more--Mignon said so. We'll free the rest someday."

"We're moving in here only because Davis left. He must be up to something. Maybe he thinks you're outside. Or maybe he's waiting for us to emerge."

Karen felt herself sliding back into the muck again. "Stop!" she shouted, "Think only of getting out--out! Do you hear me?"

"I don't have the strength," Bob whined.

"Yes, you do. You're a Kittendorf. Didn't you say this was part of your family's mission?"

"My family failed. Dundury's evil escaped causing the devastation to the South. I know what Father was trying to do now. He didn't want me to come, didn't want such things to happen again."

"Well, tough! You did come. This did happen. And, I'm here because you sent me here."

"I didn't mean to."

"Bob, I'm tired, hungry, and filthy. Think of something. *Please*!"

Bob bowed his head.

"I can't believe you," she said through the anger that filled her--and they both slid back into the muck. "Look what you did." Karen's feet sunk and stuck.

"You're on top of me again!"

"Then stand up. Dig into your memory. What were you taught? There's got to be something to use."

"The little ones might be able to help us."

"That's a great idea... why don't you ask them to help us," she said standing perfectly still.

Bob reached up for her ankle again.

"Did you notice how quiet it is," Karen said. "All the screams have stopped."

Bob's head popped through the mire. He looked around. "The light seems brighter." Straining every muscle, he pulled himself up beside her. "The light is from the little ones trying to help us. Like the firefly, reminds us to head for the light."

Dundury

"I'm dead, aren't I? "Head for the tunnel, go into the light, that's the after death experience isn't it?" Fear consumed her in the worst way.

"Karen, you're not dead."

"No, I'm dead; stuck in hell with--" She glanced at her feet.

Against all odds, he found himself smiling. "Think happy thoughts."

Karen laughed. "Will we end up in Never Land?"

"It's worth a try, don't you think? Come on."

Together they clawed and crawled through the quag, Karen thinking happy thoughts and Bob offering prayers. "We're almost there," he said. "The wall, it's getting dry and warm. Feel the difference?"

"Yes, keep going," she answered. *Christmas and summer swims, and my little calico, and Bob-- how can I be thinking about Bob?*

Thank you, God. Thank you for this woman. I love her so much.

Karen suddenly squeezed his hand so hard it hurt. "Push! We've done it!" she cried. "Look, it's morning." Tears of joy ran down her face. "We made it through the night." Laughter exploded between them. "We made it through the dark." She threw her arms around his neck.

Bob locked his lips on hers. Fire flew through her body bringing with it an incredible strength. Her arms tightened around his neck and she returned his fervor.

Pain suddenly stopped their union.

"What's the matter?"

"My hand," she said, lowering her arms and looking at her palm. "It hurts so much." The scar pulsed. "His closeness brings on the pain."

"We've got to face him."

"He's evil incarnate," Karen said.

"We'll follow the pain," he said. "It's gonna hurt you."

She closed her eyes. "Will we end up back down there--
'cause I don't think I can stand that place again."

He hugged her. "It'll be okay, Karen," he smiled. "We
know how to get out."

"He's gone home."

His eyes, full of resolve, gave her courage.

They hid at the brink of the wood that met the winding
drive to Davis' house. A ghostly figure emerged.

"That looks like Lisa."

Bob nodded.

"It is her."

Bob jumped for Lisa, dragging her back into the thicket.

"Let me go," Lisa said in a hoarse whisper.

Bob untangled the veil that clung to her leg. "Are you all
right?"

Lisa nodded. "Where's Karen?"

"I'm here, Lisa."

"He's insane," she said, panting and gasping. Lisa took
the veil out of Bob's hands and placed it on Karen's head. "He
has these little glass balls...and the book knocked on the
window, and... there was this cat--it's gone now," she said,
her head frantically moving between them and the house. "I
ran, and--"

"Calm down, Lisa. You're safe." Karen wrapped her arms
around Lisa, and patted her shoulders. "Stay out of sight while
Bob and I get Davis."

"No, not *we*, my love. It has to be me. It's my task."
Before either woman could utter a word, he was off, heading
for the front door. The book dropped out of a cloud and
landed at Karen's feet. When she tried to pick it up, a calico
paw tapped her hand, stopping her.

Chapter 18

The front door opened, just a crack, and a blast of subzero air poured out into the world. Bob felt the whoosh of evil blow over and through him.

"Don't go in there," Karen screamed.

He'd already stepped over the threshold

"I know you're here," Davis said.

Bob moved closer to the staircase.

"I also know you're not here to help me." Davis' voice thundered through the mansion. The crystal chandelier swung wildly from the ceiling; the window panes rattled, and the doors shook on their hinges.

"I can help you, Davis," Bob called.

Davis laughed. "I don't need your help, cousin. I'm pursuing my destiny--as you did yours."

Bob looked up to the second floor landing. Davis stood towering, in an almost ethereal way.

"Those stupid prayers provided your exit."

"Who prayed for us? It wasn't *you*, Davis."

"Hell forbid," he laughed. "Lisa did as it was predicted--and it hurt me."

"You can always choose another way," Bob said, slowly advancing up the stairs, one step at a time, until he reached the landing, then hesitated at the top step.

"You're afraid. I can feel your fear. It possesses you."

"Let me help you, Davis."

"How dare you presume to tell me what I need," Davis shouted. "Walk a day in my shoes! Then you'll understand," he said with contempt. "But, you felt my power," he growled. "The world is *mine* now."

"You think you have pow--"

"Shut up, you fool! I know how to use the power that has been stored for *me*," he said, beating his chest. "I can capture souls!" His black eyes sparked the bloodletting of his power. "I know how to trap the essence while I remain *above* ground."

"That power will destroy you. It's wrong--and it's the end of the world if you unleash it." Bob ventured another step toward Davis, challenging the blinding force of his stare. "It must be guarded--and cherished. You cannot play with demonology."

"It's already done," Davis said, moving along the staircase railing toward Bob

"You know it isn't. The book--"

"To hell with the book! I've figured it out. I understand all things. I can send you back to the dirt-- or straight to the pit of hell."

Bob swallowed hard. "You can't give evil a free reign."

"Why does power always have to equal evil?"

Bob bowed his head.

The house rocked.

Karen ran for the front door. It slammed shut in her face. She pounded on the door, fighting the burning ache in her hand. "Bob! Let me help you!"

Lisa came up behind her. "Karen, we must pray."

"We've gotta get in there. Davis has hold of some incredible power. He kept us under the earth. It was like being buried alive-- it was so cold and dark, with so much pain." She faced her friend. "There are things worse than death-- eternal pain and separation. Don't you understand? Davis did that to us!"

"You both got out."

Tears streamed down Karen's face as she whimpered, "He has Bob." She rubbed the aching scar in her palm; it began turning a fiery red, pulsing in the growing intensity of the pain.

"Some things must happen no matter what."

"I started all this."

"You think you have that much power?" Lisa said.

"Does Bob? Or Davis?" The house shook again knocking the women to their knees.

"Something terrible is happening," Karen said as the porch floor boards splintered, spitting the nails that held them down, they rolled across the deck and down the steps. Karen crawled back up the steps, digging her nails into the plastered column that shattered, ripping the skin from the scar on her palm. Blood gushed and spurted everywhere. "Lisa, help me."

"I'm praying. That's all I know to do to weaken Davis."

"Look at my hand," Karen panted. "It's hemorrhaging."

Lisa tore off a piece of her skirt and wrapped it around Karen's hand. "I'll put pressure on it," she said, squeezing the fabric into the wound. "Lord, help us. We need You."

Blood soaked through the fabric and puddled on the porch step. "It won't stop," Karen said, panic filling her eyes. "I'm bleeding out...I'm already dead, Lisa," she panted in the fright of what was happening to her. "We saw the light--a confused dream of Dundury," Karen said as the earth shook, rolling the women back and forth as if hell itself was bursting forth.

Lisa felt the grass crawling around her, pulling her down, close to the earth. She grabbed Karen's hand. "It's stopped bleeding--but--" Her eyes flared in unbelievable shock. "We're sinking into the soil."

"My God! Davis is pulling us under. Where are you, Bob?"

"Pray, Karen! Pray!" Lisa cried out. "I know you're scared, but *pray*!"

Drained and totally weakened, Karen lifted her head and looked into Lisa's eyes. "Pray? We're back to that again?"

"Our prayers will control Davis. Prayers make the sores come--they take his strength."

"Dammit! I've prayed all my life, and for what? The man I love is facing death from an evil force and you want me to pray," Karen screamed, lowering her head and sobbing the pain of her heart's love.

"The man you love--" Lisa said in the surprise of reality. "Do you love Bob?"

"It doesn't matter--he's in that house with Davis. And, we're sinking into the ground."

"No we're not." Lisa patted the ground. "It stopped, Karen."

Karen tentatively touched the red Georgia clay beneath her. "We can't save Bob--we can't even get up those steps," she said, wiping her tears. "You saw the glass orbs he made, they're his source of power. Davis isn't human." A sense of knowing dawned. "He's traded his soul for those glass orbs."

"They're left over from another time, along with all the evil from generations past."

"He's got reinforcements," Karen said slumping to the ground on her elbow. Mignon's veil glowed around her face. She pulled it close to her cheek.

"Losing your spunk, Karen. I thought that was why Bob sent you here?" Lisa reached out and touched the gossamer fabric; its radiance almost compelling her actions.

"He didn't send me, Bertha did."

Lisa smiled. "But, you came."

"You're a fool," Karen said, unable to look back into Lisa's eyes.

"Maybe-- but, I'm going to town and wake everybody up. We'll be at the Inn--praying."

Disbelief filled Karen. "The towns people are going to pray?"

"I've got the children. They'll all come to me."

"Maybe they'll lock you up."

"You can't help Bob. You can't even get on the porch. What else is there?"

Lisa stood up.

"I can't--" Karen cried. "I can't leave him."

Lisa bolted for the woods.

The house quaked, sending shockwaves in all directions. Davis held open the door to his bedroom. "Come, Bob, we'll talk."

Hesitation stilled Bob where he stood.

"What are ya scared of?" Davis felt a tingle run up his back; the heat was coming from a source-- *Who's praying?* He held his hand out to Bob. "Closer, cousin. Sit with me."

"I'm not afraid of you, Davis. And, you will not take my essence."

"Good! Then touch me," Davis taunted.

"So you can pull me under again?"

"*Please* touch me, *save me*," Davis mocked; his squealing laughter a demon-driven sound. "I thought you knew it all. You, the son of the great *Protector* Kittendorf. And here you are--helpless to stop all that I've discovered."

Bob stood silent watching Davis fill a crystal goblet with sherry then, Davis looked up at him.

"No. I don't think so helpless after all," he said, suddenly dropping the glass. A blister burst open in the palm of his hand. He balled his fingers into a fist--he had to hide the festering sore, otherwise, Bob would know that someone was praying.

"You going to start by punching me," Bob said, stepping into the devil's domain. Pretty balls lined the table. One lay smashed and oozing on the windowsill. "So, Lisa did break one. That's why the house is freezing."

"How many times have you faced the cold and dark, Bob?" Davis picked up the broken shards. "Want to touch *real* power? This one has the essence of Mordagar. Have you heard his name? It's in that blessed book that Lisa wants."

"No, I haven't."

"I thought you knew everything." Davis tossed the object aside. "No matter, it's gone now." He picked up another sphere and stared into it's depths. "This one is priceless--when Hitler ordered the concentration camps. Now I have his knowledge and his drive--all contained here in my little orb. This one--" he said, picking up another glass ball. "This is Machiavelli, the tutor to the world's despots. Here we have Stalin--the world's mass murderer..." He picked up yet another clear orb. "Mao Tse Tung-- another of the world's mass murderers. And, yes... here's Judas-- the Christ's betrayer... I learned a great deal from Judas--all is done with a kiss," Davis said, placing the glass spheres back into the box on the table. He leaned over the group of glowing virulence. "See how they answer me. They know who their master is."

"You're missing the small ones."

"Yes, that's right. And what do they mean?"

"They mean that somebody has been producing them... all these years," Bob said, feeling his stomach tighten.

"You mean to tell me that your pitiful family wasn't doing its job? Some tiny little evil was still at work?" Davis laughed. "C'mon, Bobby, what do these little balls *really* signify?"

Bob blanched.

Dundury

"And the cat came back the very next day," Davis mocked, singing the children's rhyme.

Came back... Bob stood silent, his face reflecting horror.

"That's right! My dear old Dad melted in the woods...gone forever. Not!" Davis pressed closer. "You were so cute telling Karen about me and those sores; worried about my demise--and so afraid that I'd end up like my *father*."

"Your father was sent to hell."

"So were you and Karen, but you both crawled out."

"Oh, God! Oh, God," Bob said.

"Praying, Bob?" Davis asked, leering and taking another step closer to Bob. A spot of flesh on his cheek glowed red, the skin broke apart as it began to melt.

Bob took a breath.

"Pray all you want, fool," Davis sneered. "It's their fear--"

"You know so much, Davis. Tell me," Bob said.

"Mankind has much to fear. When the time of judgment nears, they look to the heavens. When death is upon them, the sunrise matters. People in crisis fear the Lord...it is then that they make their deal with the devil."

Bob stood shaking his head. Then he smiled. It was a deliberate move. "You fool...you got those sores because Grace served up your retribution. And then, who touched you to *stop* the sores, Davis--*who?*" Bob continued, refusing Davis his say. "Karen stopped the sores--because her essence is good--it's pure--and you'll never know, or possess it in your present state of heart and soul. *Never*, you fool!"

Davis doubled over with laughter, his ploy to stall for time as he thought to reason a reply. "No! It was my essence *with* hers that stopped the sores."

"You lie, Davis."

"They look to cards and magic, shamans and fortune tellers."

"So what made Philip--your grandfather--reappear and breed you?"

Davis snickered. "Maybe he thought happy thoughts like you and your bimbo." Davis felt his power growing through his hate; the intensity of his demented beliefs had sustained him. Nothing anyone said would deter him.

"Your family line is only happy when it's stirring up trouble," Bob said.

"*Trouble*? My dear cousin. Maybe your precious granny gave away too much."

"Your father was consumed in his own curse. Remember the little girls--Mignon and Bertha--and what they said? *The sores began first in your father's soul.*"

"My father lived for the glory, like everyone else."

Bob shook his head. "You'll never understand, Davis."

"I understand that mankind wants power. Sherman got that. He'll always be remembered."

"Because he ventured too far."

"He played the pawn and, in return, received his infamy. He had his turn, then gave his essence back to my father," Davis said proudly.

"It was your father's evil--"

"Yes! It was! He existed for a while in the underworld where he practiced the arts. But my father was allowed back into the world," he said. The walls began to bow and weave with the slithering sound of Davis' voice.

"Well, since he blew it the first time--"

Davis snickered. "Do you know what year heralded his return?" Davis looked at his flesh; ripples pulsing as it began disintegrating. "1960. Can you guess why?"

Bob watched Davis as he pranced back to the table.

"Remember the riots...the Vietnam quagmire and the dissention in the country? And, lest we forget JFK's assassination!" He stood arrogantly challenging Bob to the reality of the power his father had mastered. "I've got the powders and potions. They're all measured out."

"You're not your father. And I won't let you play this

game," Bob said, rushing at Davis, and flipping over the table, heaving his full weight and crashing head on into Davis.

The box of orbs sailed into the air. Suspended, floating momentarily, and then, each of the glass spheres exploded. The dust blew out in all directions, sifting through the air and, finally, floating down onto the polished floor. In the instant that the dust settled, the boards began to smoke, sizzling as they melted giving way to a massive hole in the floor.

Bob blinked and the joist gave way, exposing the floor down on the first level. Its boards also crackling under an unseen heat that dissolved the pine flooring all the way through to the dirt foundation below the house. The black hole deepened and with each moment, a creeping vile stench drifted up from the pit. "It's returning to the earth. Maybe there's another whose return is now," Bob screamed.

"No!" Davis shouted. His head swiveled in contortions of demonic proportions while his eyes blazed a black more hideous than Bob had ever seen. "I've taken care of everything," Davis screamed, unclenching his fist.

"I see the sores, Davis. Some of us still know how to pray."

"But, not enough, Bob. Never enough," Davis shouted and the foundation rocked its consent. "I am the *only* lord now."

Bob stepped closer. "Are you sure? The book is gone from you."

"No, I feel it. I know it cover to cover. All the prophecy-- the power--it's *mine* now."

"You've discovered how to bring the pages out," Bob challenged him.

"Maybe I've rewritten the work."

"You can't change it-- it is as it was in the beginning. It allows only that you choose your path."

"And you chose to be the hero?"

"I chose to follow the *truth*."

"Because it gives you power? You're a pitiful man in love

with a woman who won't have you, a magazine that's going nowhere--and the secrets of Dundury that you're scarred shitless to use." Davis charged, in his contempt for Bob.

Bob shook his head. Then, with a deliberate and reverent intent, he shook the dust from his shoes--and waited.

Davis sneered, then screamed out as the sores rapidly began multiplying, each one bubbling his skin in the insatiable appetite of their consumption.

"Better to reign in hell than serve in heaven? Is that your plan, Davis? It didn't work then, it doesn't work now, and it never will work."

"I can crush you, you sniveling bastard!" He howled, stretching and gyrating to the chanting incantations that bubbled up from the chasm below them. "Did you enjoy the humidor? Did the darkness fit your mood?"

"Father to son, twice four to eight..." Bob said, repeating his own incantation.

"You don't have the measures, or the power."

"Before it's too late, too late, too late," Bob said, ignoring Davis, and extending his hand over the pit that the orbs had made. One by one they returned, levitating in the air. *"The prayers of the people, save one for each other, one and all. Children and roses, cats and claws, one for each other, one and all."* The spheres began spinning, glowing in intensity, and coming to rest side by side encircling Bob's feet. He glanced up at Davis. "Are you sure of who the master really is?"

Davis stood speechless, his face a mask of confusion. "How did you call them?" Davis leaned over to scoop up the orbs. "They're mine, my collection, my hope, *my power*," he warned, advancing on Bob who stood beyond the abyss.

"I feel the prayers too, Davis. What weakens you strengthens me. So many told me I was inept. The one person who always loved and supported me was Bertha--and you took her from me. You'll take no one else," Bob said, kicking a single glass ball; it started a chain reaction; each orb dropping into the pit from whence it had returned.

Davis cocked his head, scratched the disintegrating skin on his face, and flung the rotting flesh at Bob. It hung suspended in mid air. He took a step and the floor boards cracked beneath his weight. Bob grabbed for Davis, but the prayers had been answered.

Davis dissolved before Bob's eyes; his bones disengaging from his skeletal frame on its descent into hell.

Bob scraped his shoe against the remaining powder. "Evil to evil, dust to dust."

Little flickers of light coalesced around him. "My fairies, welcome to the world," he said, his hand gently reaching into the caressing light, as the morning sun draping him with a renewing warmth.

"It's finished," Bob said and walked out of the room.

Karen lay crying in a crumpled heap in the front yard. The Book sat in her lap and on top of it, the calico cat.

Bob sat down on the grass beside her. "What's the matter, honey?"

"My friend is in that place with the devil. I can't even get up the steps." Heartbreaking sobs punctuated her words. "I love him so much. I never knew how much-- and now he's--"

"He's here, Karen."

She sat up; incredulity covered her tear-laddened face. "My God! You're alive!"

"I guess I was the strongest," he said, shrugging his shoulders in his adorably humble way.

"Is it *really* over?" Karen asked.

"For a time," he said, folding his arms around her and tucking her close to him. "Why are you wearing a wedding veil?"

"I think it was Mignon's."

"Hmm..." He hugged her tightly.

"I don't think it's a wedding veil," she said. "I guess it could be," she hesitated. "If someone had a reason."

"Are you hinting?" Bob chided her.

She lifted herself off his chest. "Of course not! I've known you too long. We'd never make a couple. You don't even like cats and now here's another one to take home." She stroked the cat as it climbed onto her lap. "I hope Calico will like her."

"What will you call her? Surely you can't call the two cats *Calico*. They'd be terribly confused."

Karen opened the Book to the first page. "Maybe I'll find an appropriate name in here."

"Can you see the words now?"

"Yes, but," she paled, "I've seen them before." Her fingers flipped page after page, her mind growing cloudy.

"It's all been said before, Karen, only nobody listened."

She turned back to the first words. "The first line reads... *In the beginning...*"

"I know what it says."

"But it's not the same as before."

"I thought the pages were blank before."

"Yes, but the pictures and the light. It talked about fathers and sons and... "The cat squirmed. "I don't get it."

Bob fluffed the veil around her head, then helped her to her feet. He scratched the cat under its chin. "These animals really are soothing aren't they?"

"Don't change the subject."

"What subject?"

Karen shook her head. "What happened to Davis?"

"He's gone."

"Gone where?"

"I don't know. Let it be enough that we're safe and can go home now," he said, then kissed her cheek. "Where's Lisa?"

"She went back to Dundury. She was going to wake up

the whole town and have some sort of prayer session."

"Oh, so that's what happened," Bob said. "Don't you think we should join her? It is a beautiful morning."

"What about the story? What about all that's happened here? It needs to be told, Bob." She fell silent, for only a moment, then looked into his eyes. "Can we tell it?"

"Sure, the Inn is lovely and tourists will liven up Dundury," he said. "Of course, we'll have to get the State Legislature to put it back on the map."

"That's not what I mean. *All of it*-- can we tell it all?"

"It wouldn't matter, Karen. People don't want to face the reality of evil. It's a hidden enemy that rides on the wings of the familiar. That's where it draws its strength. Dundury is a pretty little town, full of pretty houses, and pretty people. Fairy tales are fine, until they turn ugly. For now, Davis is where he was destined to be. Dundury will survive in its own way, and we can get on with our lives."

"Is that a *no*?"

You'll forget what happened here."

"Not as long as I have this," Karen said, holding up her scarred hand.

His brow lifted. "Looking after two cats, you probably will forget. I pray you do forget."

"I came for a story, and I found one. It's got to be told."

"It's over, Karen," he said, looking deep into her eyes.

"Alright...but, I'm going back into town one more time."

His look mesmerized her, she *felt* it, longed for it.

"Lisa went to pray. I think it's time I joined her."

"You? Pray?" he asked through a smile that took full possession of his lips.

Karen's lips broke into a delicate grin and she adjusted the veil on her head. "Coming with me?"

"Yes," Bob said, curling his arm around her waist. "I'm with you, honey."

Ava Lindsey Chambers

Dundury

Epilogue

Bob got out of his car and slowly walked the drive around to the front of his office. He lifted the mail out of the mailbox and shoved it under his arm, several large envelopes and a small box dropped to the pavement. "That's nice," he muttered.

He scooped up the fallen pieces, unlocked the door and went inside. Inside was dark, as usual, and he dug into his jacket pocket for the lighter. He climbed the stairs, pausing to light every candle he could find. His nose wrinkled as he pushed open the door to his office that smelled musty and unused. He threw the mail on his desk, lit the rest of the candles, and slid open the curtains on the window. Looking out into the dawn, he fought his mind for reason. The ringing phone startled him.

"Hello."

"Hi, Bob, it's me, Karen. I love the little calico you found me. She's awfully feisty and wants to be held all the time. She even scratched me, the little tiger."

"Oh?"

"Yeah, put a long gash in the palm of my hand. I think it'll leave a scar."

"And you still want to keep her?"

"She needs me."

"I'm sure she does," Bob said.

"Where's Bertha? I expected her to give me a hard time."

Sadness filled him. "She left to be with her sister, remember?"

"Did you tell me that? I guess I forgot. Anyway, just open the present I sent you."

"Present?"

"Yeah, it's not much. I found it in an antique store. Open it and call me later. We'll meet for lunch."

"Sure," he said, hanging up the phone. He sat down behind his desk and the pile of morning mail. He found the box with Karen's return address.

It worked, he thought. *She doesn't remember a thing. Good ole calico did her work.*

He stared at the box. "Oh Bertha, I tried not to do it. I didn't want to."

A voice answered him. "It is as it was meant to be."

He shrugged off his melancholy and opened the box. The tissue paper wrapping glowed. He lifted the paper and fell back in his chair. His hands began to shake as he unfolded the paper. A beautiful glass paperweight sat snugly and warmly in the little box.

Why would you send me this, Karen?

"It is as it was meant to be," the gentle voice reminded him.

Dundury

To be continued...

Ava Lindsey Chambers

Dundury

INSTRUCTIONS FOR THE GOVERNMENT OF ARMIES OF THE UNITED STATES IN THE FIELD

Prepared by Francis Lieber, promulgated as General Orders No. 100 by President Lincoln, 24 April 1863.

The text below is reprinted from the edition of the United States Government Printing Office of 1898; and reprinted in Schindler & Toman,eds., The Laws of Armed Confllicts

Instructions for the Government of Armies of the United States in the Field, prepared by Francis Lieber, LL.D., Originally Issued as **General Orders No. 100**, Adjutant General's Office, 1863, Washington 1898:Government Printing Office.

TABLE OF CONTENTS
Articles

SECTION I
Martial Law - Military jurisdiction - Military necessity - Retaliation

Article 1. A place, district, or country occupied by an enemy stands, in consequence of the occupation, under the Martial Law of the invading or occupying army, whether any proclamation declaring Martial Law, or any public warning to the inhabitants, has been issued or not. Martial Law is the immediate and direct effect and consequence of occupation or conquest.

The presence of a hostile army proclaims its Martial Law.

Art. 2. Martial Law does not cease during the hostile occupation, except by special proclamation, ordered by the commander in chief; or by special mention in the treaty of peace concluding the war, when the occupation of a place or territory continues beyond the conclusion of peace as one of the conditions of the same.

Art. 3. Martial Law in a hostile country consists in the suspension, by the occupying military authority, of the criminal and civil law, and of the domestic administration and government in the occupied place or territory, and in the substitution of military rule and force for the same, as well as in the dictation of general laws, as far as military necessity requires this suspension, substitution, or dictation.

The commander of the forces may proclaim that the administration of all civil and penal law shall continue either wholly or in part, as in times of peace, unless otherwise ordered by the military authority.

Art. 4. Martial Law is simply military authority exercised in accordance with the laws and usages of war. Military oppression is not Martial Law: it is the abuse of the power which that law confers. As Martial Law is executed by military force, it is incumbent upon those who administer it to be strictly guided by the principles of justice, honor, and humanity - virtues adorning a soldier even more than other men, for the very reason that he possesses the power of his arms against the unarmed.

Art. 5. Martial Law should be less stringent in places and countries fully occupied and fairly conquered. Much greater severity may be exercised in places or regions where actual hostilities exist, or are expected and must be prepared for. Its most complete sway is allowed - even in the commander's own country - when face to face with the enemy, because of the absolute necessities of the case, and of the paramount duty to defend the country against invasion.

To save the country is paramount to all other considerations.

Art. 6. All civil and penal law shall continue to take its usual course in the enemy's places and territories under Martial Law, unless interrupted or stopped by order of the occupying military power; but all the functions of the hostile government - legislative executive, or administrative - whether of a general, provincial, or local character, cease under Martial Law, or continue only with the sanction, or, if deemed necessary, the participation of the occupier or invader.

Art. 7. Martial Law extends to property, and to persons, whether they are subjects of the enemy or aliens to that government.

Art. 8. Consuls, among American and European nations, are not diplomatic agents. Nevertheless, their offices and persons will be subjected to Martial Law in cases of urgent necessity only: their property and business are not exempted. Any delinquency they commit against the established military rule may be punished as in the case of any other inhabitant, and such punishment furnishes no reasonable ground for international complaint.

Art. 9. The functions of Ambassadors, Ministers, or other diplomatic agents accredited by neutral powers to the hostile government, cease, so far as regards the displaced government; but the conquering or occupying power usually recognizes them as temporarily accredited to itself.

Art. 10. Martial Law affects chiefly the police and collection of public revenue and taxes, whether imposed by the expelled government or by the invader, and refers mainly to the support and efficiency of the army, its safety, and the safety of its operations.

Art. 11. The law of war does not only disclaim all cruelty and bad faith concerning engagements concluded with the enemy during the war, but also the breaking of stipulations solemnly contracted by the belligerents in time of peace, and avowedly intended to remain in force in case of war between the contracting powers.

It disclaims all extortions and other transactions for individual gain; all acts of private revenge, or connivance at such acts.

Offenses to the contrary shall be severely punished, and especially so if committed by officers.

Art. 12. Whenever feasible, Martial Law is carried out in cases of individual offenders by Military Courts; but sentences of death shall be executed only with the approval of the chief executive, provided the urgency of the case does not require a speedier execution, and then only with the approval of the chief commander.

Art. 13. Military jurisdiction is of two kinds: First, that which is conferred and defined by statute; second, that which is derived from the common law of war. Military offenses under the statute law must be tried in the manner therein directed; but military offenses which do not come within the statute must be tried and punished under the common law of war. The character of the courts which exercise these jurisdictions depends upon the local laws of each particular country.

In the armies of the United States the first is exercised by courts-martial, while cases which do not come within the "Rules and Articles of War," or the jurisdiction conferred by statute on courts-martial, are tried by military commissions.

Art. 14. Military necessity, as understood by modern civilized nations, consists in the necessity of those measures which are indispensable for securing the ends of the war, and which are lawful according to the modern law and usages of war.

Art. 15. Military necessity admits of all direct destruction of life or limb of armed enemies, and of other persons whose destruction is incidentally unavoidable in the armed contests of the war; it allows of the capturing of every armed enemy, and every enemy of importance to the hostile government, or of peculiar danger to the captor; it allows of all destruction of property, and obstruction of the ways and channels of traffic, travel, or communication, and of all withholding of sustenance or means of life from the enemy; of the appropriation of whatever an enemy's country affords necessary for the subsistence and safety of the army, and of such deception as does not involve the breaking of good faith either positively pledged, regarding agreements entered into during the war, or supposed by the modern law of war to exist. Men who take up arms against one another in public war do not cease on this account to be moral beings, responsible to one another and to God.

Art. 16. *Military necessity does not admit of cruelty - that is, the infliction of suffering for the sake of suffering or for revenge, nor of maiming or wounding except in fight, nor of* torture to extort confessions. It does not admit of the use of poison in any way, *nor of the wanton devastation of a district.* It admits of deception, but disclaims acts of perfidy; and, in general, *military necessity does not include any act of hostility which makes the return to peace unnecessarily difficult.*

Art. 17. War is not carried on by arms alone. It is lawful to starve the hostile belligerent, armed or unarmed, so that it leads to the speedier subjection of the enemy.

Art. 18. When a commander of a besieged place expels the noncombatants, in order to lessen the number of those who consume his stock of provisions, it is lawful, though an extreme measure, to drive them back, so as to hasten on the surrender.

Art. 19. Commanders, whenever admissible, inform the enemy of their intention to bombard a place, so that the noncombatants, and especially the women and children, may be removed before the bombardment commences. But it is no infraction of the common law of war to omit thus to inform the enemy. Surprise may be a necessity.

Art. 20. Public war is a state of armed hostility between sovereign nations or governments. It is a law and requisite of civilized existence that men live in political, continuous societies, forming organized units, called states or nations, whose constituents bear, enjoy, suffer, advance and retrograde together, in peace and in war.

Art. 21. The citizen or native of a hostile country is thus an enemy, as one of the constituents of the hostile state or nation, and as such is subjected to the hardships of the war.

Art. 22. Nevertheless, as civilization has advanced during the last centuries, so has likewise steadily advanced, especially in war on land, the distinction between the private individual belonging to a hostile country and the hostile country itself, with its men in arms. The principle has been more and more acknowledged that the unarmed citizen is to be spared in person, property, and honor as much as the exigencies of war will admit.

Art. 23. Private citizens are no longer murdered, enslaved, or carried off to distant parts, and the inoffensive individual is as little disturbed in his private relations as the commander of the hostile troops can afford to grant in the overruling demands of a vigorous war.

Art. 24. The almost universal rule in remote times was, and continues to be with barbarous armies, that the private individual of the hostile country is destined to suffer every privation of liberty and protection, and every disruption of family ties. Protection was, and still is with uncivilized people, the exception.

Art. 25. In modern regular wars of the Europeans, and their descendants in other portions of the globe, protection of the inoffensive citizen of the hostile country is the rule; privation and disturbance of private relations are the exceptions.

Art. 26. Commanding generals may cause the magistrates and civil officers of the hostile country to take the oath of temporary allegiance or an oath of fidelity to their own victorious government or rulers, and they may expel everyone who declines to do so. But whether they do so or not, the people and their civil officers owe strict obedience to them as long as they hold sway over the district or country, at the peril of their lives.

Art. 27. The law of war can no more wholly dispense with retaliation than can the law of nations, of which it is a branch. Yet civilized nations acknowledge retaliation as the sternest feature of war. A reckless enemy often leaves to his opponent no other means of securing himself against the repetition of barbarous outrage

Art. 28. Retaliation will, therefore, never be resorted to as a measure of mere revenge, but only as a means of protective retribution, and moreover, cautiously and unavoidably; that is to say, retaliation shall only be resorted to after careful inquiry into the real occurrence, and the character of the misdeeds that may demand retribution.

Unjust or inconsiderate retaliation removes the belligerents farther and farther from the mitigating rules of regular war, and by rapid steps leads them nearer to the internecine wars of savages.

Art. 29. Modern times are distinguished from earlier ages by the existence, at one and the same time, of many nations and great governments related to one another in close intercourse.

Peace is their normal condition; war is the exception. The ultimate object of all modern war is a renewed state of peace.

The more vigorously wars are pursued, the better it is for humanity. Sharp wars are brief.

Art. 30. Ever since the formation and coexistence of modern nations, and ever since wars have become great national wars, war has come to be acknowledged not to be its own end, but the means to obtain great ends of state, or to consist in defense against wrong; and no conventional restriction of the modes adopted to injure the enemy is any longer admitted; but the law of war imposes many limitations and restrictions on principles of justice, faith, and honor.

SECTION II

Public and private property of the enemy - Protection of persons, and especially of women, of religion, the arts and sciences - Punishment of crimes against the inhabitants of hostile countries.

Dundury

Art. 31. A victorious army appropriates all public money, seizes all public movable property until further direction by its government, and sequesters for its own benefit or of that of its government all the revenues of real property belonging to the hostile government or nation. The title to such real property remains in abeyance during military occupation, and until the conquest is made complete.

Art. 32. A victorious army, by the martial power inherent in the same, may suspend, change, or abolish, as far as the martial power extends, the relations which arise from the services due, according to the existing laws of the invaded country, from one citizen, subject, or native of the same to another.

The commander of the army must leave it to the ultimate treaty of peace to settle the permanency of this change.

Art. 33. It is no longer considered lawful - on the contrary, it is held to be a serious breach of the law of war - to force the subjects of the enemy into the service of the victorious government, except the latter should proclaim, after a fair and complete conquest of the hostile country or district, that it is resolved to keep the country, district, or place permanently as its own and make it a portion of its own country.

Art. 34. As a general rule, the property belonging to churches, to hospitals, or other establishments of an exclusively charitable character, to establishments of education, or foundations for the promotion of knowledge, whether public schools, universities, academies of learning or observatories, museums of the fine arts, or of a scientific character such property is not to be considered public property in the sense of paragraph 31; but it may be taxed or used when the public service may require it.

Art. 35. Classical works of art, libraries, scientific collections, or precious instruments, such as astronomical telescopes, as well as hospitals, must be secured against all avoidable injury, even when they are contained in fortified places whilst besieged or bombarded.

Art. 36. If such works of art, libraries, collections, or instruments belonging to a hostile nation or government, can be removed without injury, the ruler of the conquering state or nation may order them to be seized and removed for the benefit of the said nation. The ultimate ownership is to be settled by the ensuing treaty of peace.

In no case shall they be sold or given away, if captured by the armies of the United States, nor shall they ever be privately appropriated, or wantonly destroyed or injured.

Art. 37. The United States acknowledge and protect, in hostile countries occupied by them, religion and morality; strictly private property; the persons of the inhabitants, especially those of women: and the sacredness of domestic relations. Offenses to the contrary shall be rigorously punished.

This rule does not interfere with the right of the victorious invader to tax the people or their property, to levy forced loans, to billet soldiers, or to appropriate property, especially houses, lands, boats or ships, and churches, for temporary and military uses

Art. 38. Private property, unless forfeited by crimes or by offenses of the owner, can be seized only by way of military necessity, for the support or other benefit of the army or of the United States.
If the owner has not fled, the commanding officer will cause receipts to be given, which may serve the spoliated owner to obtain indemnity.

Art. 39. The salaries of civil officers of the hostile government who remain in the invaded territory, and continue the work of their office, and can continue it according to the circumstances arising out of the war-such as judges, administrative or police officers, officers of city or communal governments - are paid from the public revenue of the invaded territory, until the military government has reason wholly or partially to discontinue it. Salaries or incomes connected with purely honorary titles are always stopped.

Art. 40. There exists no law or body of authoritative rules of action between hostile armies, except that branch of the law of nature and nations which is called the law and usages of war on land.

Art. 41. All municipal law of the ground on which the armies stand, or of the countries to which they belong, is silent and of no effect between armies in the field.

Art. 42. Slavery, complicating and confounding the ideas of property, (that is of a thing,) and of personality, (that is of humanity,) exists according to municipal or local law only. The law of nature and nations has never acknowledged it. The digest of the Roman law enacts the early dictum of the pagan jurist, that "so far as the law of nature is concerned, all men are equal." Fugitives escaping from a country in which they were slaves, villains, or serfs, into another country, have, for centuries past, been held free and acknowledged free by judicial decisions of European countries, even though the municipal law of the country in which the slave had taken refuge acknowledged slavery within its own dominions.

Art. 43. Therefore, in a war between the United States and a belligerent which admits of slavery, if a person held in bondage by that belligerent be captured by or come as a fugitive under the protection of the military forces of the United States, such person is immediately entitled to the rights and privileges of a freeman. To return such person into slavery would amount to enslaving a free person, and neither the United States nor any officer under their authority can enslave any human being. Moreover, a person so made free by the law of war is under the shield of the law of nations, and the former owner or State can have, by the law of postliminy, no belligerent lien or claim of service.

Art. 44. All wanton violence committed against persons in the invaded country, all destruction of property not commanded by the authorized officer, all robbery, all pillage or sacking, even after taking a place by main force, all rape, wounding, maiming, or killing of such inhabitants, are prohibited under the penalty of death, or such other severe punishment as may seem adequate for the gravity of the offense.

A soldier, officer or private, in the act of committing such violence, and disobeying a superior ordering him to abstain from it, may be lawfully killed on the spot by such superior.

Art. 45. All captures and booty belong, according to the modern law of war, primarily to the government of the captor.

Prize money, whether on sea or land, can now only be claimed under local law.

Art. 46. Neither officers nor soldiers are allowed to make use of their position or power in the hostile country for private gain, not even for commercial transactions otherwise legitimate. Offenses to the contrary committed by commissioned officers will be punished with cashiering or such other punishment as the nature of the offense may require; if by soldiers, they shall be punished according to the nature of the offense.

Art. 47. Crimes punishable by all penal codes, such as arson, murder, maiming, assaults, highway robbery, theft, burglary, fraud, forgery, and rape, if committed by an American soldier in a hostile country against its inhabitants, are not only punishable as at home, but in all cases in which death is not inflicted, the severer punishment shall be preferred.

SECTION III
Deserters - Prisoners of war - Hostages - Booty on the battle-field.

Art. 48. Deserters from the American Army, having entered the service of the enemy, suffer death if they fall again into the hands of the United States, whether by capture, or being delivered up to the American Army; and if a deserter from the enemy, having taken service in the Army of the United States, is captured by the enemy, and punished by them with death or otherwise, it is not a breach against the law and usages of war, requiring redress or retaliation.

Art. 49. A prisoner of war is a public enemy armed or attached to the hostile army for active aid, who has fallen into the hands of the captor, either fighting or wounded, on the field or in the hospital, by individual surrender or by capitulation.

All soldiers, of whatever species of arms; all men who belong to the rising en masse of the hostile country; all those who are attached to the army for its efficiency and promote directly the object of the war, except such as are hereinafter provided for; all disabled men or officers on the field or elsewhere, if captured; all enemies who have thrown away their arms and ask for quarter, are prisoners of war, and as such exposed to the inconveniences as well as entitled to the privileges of a prisoner of war.

Art. 50. Moreover, citizens who accompany an army for whatever purpose, such as sutlers, editors, or reporters of journals, or contractors, if captured, may be made prisoners of war, and be detained as such.

The monarch and members of the hostile reigning family,

male or female, the chief, and chief officers of the hostile government, its diplomatic agents, and all persons who are of particular and singular use and benefit to the hostile army or its government, are, if captured on belligerent ground, and if unprovided with a safe conduct granted by the captor's government, prisoners of war.

Art. 51. If the people of that portion of an invaded country which is not yet occupied by the enemy, or of the whole country, at the approach of a hostile army, rise, under a duly authorized levy en masse to resist the invader, they are now treated as public enemies, and, if captured, are prisoners of war.

Art. 52. No belligerent has the right to declare that he will treat every captured man in arms of a levy en masse as a brigand or bandit. If, however, the people of a country, or any portion of the same, already occupied by an army, rise against it, they are violators of the laws of war, and are not entitled to their protection.

Art. 53. The enemy's chaplains, officers of the medical staff, apothecaries, hospital nurses and servants, if they fall into the hands of the American Army, are not prisoners of war, unless the commander has reasons to retain them. In this latter case; or if, at their own desire, they are allowed to remain with their captured companions, they are treated as prisoners of war, and may be exchanged if the commander sees fit.

Art. 54. A hostage is a person accepted as a pledge for the fulfillment of an agreement concluded between belligerents during the war, or in consequence of a war. Hostages are rare in the present age.

Art. 55. If a hostage is accepted, he is treated like a prisoner of war, according to rank and condition, as circumstances may admit.

Art. 56. A prisoner of war is subject to no punishment for being a public enemy, nor is any revenge wreaked upon him by the intentional infliction of any suffering, or disgrace, by cruel imprisonment, want of food, by mutilation, death, or any other barbarity.

Art. 57. So soon as a man is armed by a sovereign government and takes the soldier's oath of fidelity, he is a belligerent; his killing, wounding, or other warlike acts are not individual crimes or offenses. No belligerent has a right to declare that enemies of a certain class, color, or condition, when properly organized as soldiers, will not be treated by him as public enemies.

Art. 58. The law of nations knows of no distinction of color, and if an enemy of the United States should enslave and sell any captured persons of their army, it would be a case for the severest retaliation, if not redressed upon complaint.

The United States cannot retaliate by enslavement; therefore death must be the retaliation for this crime against the law of nations.

Art. 59. A prisoner of war remains answerable for his crimes committed against the captor's army or people, committed before he was captured, and for which he has not been punished by his own authorities.

All prisoners of war are liable to the infliction of retaliatory measures.

Art. 60. It is against the usage of modern war to resolve, in hatred and revenge, to give no quarter. No body of troops has the right to declare that it will not give, and therefore will not expect, quarter; but a commander is permitted to direct his troops to give no quarter, in great straits, when his own salvation makes it impossible to cumber himself with prisoners.

Art. 61. Troops that give no quarter have no right to kill enemies already disabled on the ground, or prisoners captured by other troops.

Art. 62. All troops of the enemy known or discovered to give no quarter in general, or to any portion of the army, receive none.

Art. 63. Troops who fight in the uniform of their enemies, without any plain, striking, and uniform mark of distinction of their own, can expect no quarter.

Art. 64. If American troops capture a train containing uniforms of the enemy, and the commander considers it advisable to distribute them for use among his men, some striking mark or sign must be adopted to distinguish the American soldier from the enemy.

Art. 65. The use of the enemy's national standard, flag, or other emblem of nationality, for the purpose of deceiving the enemy in battle, is an act of perfidy by which they lose all claim to the protection of the laws of war.

Art. 66. Quarter having been given to an enemy by American troops, under a misapprehension of his true character, he may, nevertheless, be ordered to suffer death if, within three days after the battle, it be discovered that he belongs to a corps which gives no quarter.

Art. 67. The law of nations allows every sovereign government to make war upon another sovereign state, and, therefore, admits of no rules or laws different from those of regular warfare, regarding the treatment of prisoners of war, although they may belong to the army of a government which the captor may consider as a wanton and unjust assailant.

Art. 68. Modern wars are not internecine wars, in which the killing of the enemy is the object. The destruction of the enemy in modern war, and, indeed, modern war itself, are means to obtain that object of the belligerent which lies beyond the war.

Unnecessary or revengeful destruction of life is not lawful.

Art. 69. Outposts, sentinels, or pickets are not to be fired upon, except to drive them in, or when a positive order, special or general, has been issued to that effect.

Art. 70. The use of poison in any manner, be it to poison wells, or food, or arms, is wholly excluded from modern warfare. He that uses it puts himself out of the pale of the law and usages of war.

Art.71. Whoever intentionally inflicts additional wounds on an enemy already wholly disabled, or kills such an enemy, or who orders or encourages soldiers to do so, shall suffer death, if duly convicted, whether he belongs to the Army of the United States, or is an enemy captured after having committed his misdeed.

Art. 72. Money and other valuables on the person of a prisoner, such as watches or jewelry, as well as extra clothing, are regarded by the American Army as the private property of the prisoner, and the appropriation of such valuables or money is considered dishonorable, and is prohibited. Nevertheless, if large sums are found upon the persons of prisoners, or in their possession, they shall be taken from them, and the surplus, after providing for their own support, appropriated for the use of the army, under the direction of the commander, unless otherwise ordered by the government. Nor can prisoners claim, as private property, large sums found and captured in their train, although they have been placed in the private luggage of the prisoners.

Art. 73. All officers, when captured, must surrender their side arms to the captor. They may be restored to the prisoner in marked cases, by the commander, to signalize admiration of his distinguished bravery or approbation of his humane treatment of prisoners before his capture. The captured officer to whom they may be restored can not wear them during captivity.

Art. 74. A prisoner of war, being a public enemy, is the prisoner of the government, and not of the captor. No ransom can be paid by a prisoner of war to his individual captor or to any officer in command. The government alone releases captives, according to rules prescribed by itself.

Art. 75. Prisoners of war are subject to confinement or imprisonment such as may be deemed necessary on account of safety, but they are to be subjected to no other intentional suffering or indignity. The confinement and mode of treating a prisoner may be varied during his captivity according to the demands of safety.

Art. 76. Prisoners of war shall be fed upon plain and wholesome food, whenever practicable, and treated with humanity.

They may be required to work for the benefit of the captor's government, according to their rank and condition.

Art. 77. A prisoner of war who escapes may be shot or otherwise killed in his flight; but neither death nor any other punishment shall be inflicted upon him simply for his attempt to escape, which the law of war does not consider a crime. Stricter means of security shall be used after an unsuccessful attempt at escape.

If, however, a conspiracy is discovered, the purpose of which is a united or general escape, the conspirators may be rigorously punished, even with death; and capital punishment may also be inflicted upon prisoners of war discovered to have plotted rebellion against the authorities of the captors, whether in union with fellow prisoners or other persons.

Art. 78. If prisoners of war, having given no pledge nor made any promise on their honor, forcibly or otherwise escape, and are captured again in battle after having rejoined their own army, they shall not be punished for their escape, but shall be treated as simple prisoners of war, although they will be subjected to stricter confinement.

Art. 79. Every captured wounded enemy shall be medically treated, according to the ability of the medical staff.

Art. 80. Honorable men, when captured, will abstain from giving to the enemy information concerning their own army, and the modern law of war permits no longer the use of any violence against prisoners in order to extort the desired information or to punish them for having given false information.

SECTION IV

Partisans - Armed enemies not belonging to the hostile army - Scouts - Armed prowlers - War-rebels

Art. 81. Partisans are soldiers armed and wearing the uniform of their army, but belonging to a corps which acts detached from the main body for the purpose of making inroads into the territory occupied by the enemy. If captured, they are entitled to all the privileges of the prisoner of war.

Art. 82. Men, or squads of men, who commit hostilities, whether by fighting, or inroads for destruction or plunder, or by raids of any kind, without commission, without being part and portion of the organized hostile army, and without sharing continuously in the war, but who do so with intermitting returns to their homes and avocations, or with the occasional assumption of the semblance of peaceful pursuits, divesting themselves of the character or appearance of soldiers - such men, or squads of men, are not public enemies, and, therefore, if captured, are not entitled to the privileges of prisoners of war, but shall be treated summarily as highway robbers or pirates.

Art. 83. Scouts, or single soldiers, if disguised in the dress of the country or in the uniform of the army hostile to their own, employed in obtaining information, if found within or lurking about the lines of the captor, are treated as spies, and suffer death.

Art. 84. Armed prowlers, by whatever names they may be called, or persons of the enemy's territory, who steal within the lines of the hostile army for the purpose of robbing, killing, or of destroying bridges, roads or canals, or of robbing or destroying the mail, or of cutting the telegraph wires, are not entitled to the privileges of the prisoner of war.

Art. 85. War-rebels are persons within an occupied territory who rise in arms against the occupying or conquering army, or against the authorities established by the same. If captured, they may suffer death, whether they rise singly, in small or large bands, and whether called upon to do so by their own, but expelled, government or not. They are not prisoners of war; nor are they if discovered and secured before their conspiracy has matured to an actual rising or armed violence.

SECTION V
Safe-conduct - Spies - War-traitors - Captured messengers - Abuse of the flag of truce

Art. 86. All intercourse between the territories occupied by belligerent armies, whether by traffic, by letter, by travel, or in any other way, ceases. This is the general rule, to be observed without special proclamation.

Exceptions to this rule, whether by safe-conduct, or permission to trade on a small or large scale, or by exchanging mails, or by travel from one territory into the other, can take place only according to agreement approved by the government, or by the highest military authority.

Contraventions of this rule are highly punishable.

Art. 87. Ambassadors, and all other diplomatic agents of neutral powers, accredited to the enemy, may receive safe-conducts through the territories occupied by the belligerents, unless there are military reasons to the contrary, and unless they may reach the place of their destination conveniently by another route. It implies no international affront if the safe-conduct is declined. Such passes are usually given by the supreme authority of the State, and not by subordinate officers.

Art. 88. A spy is a person who secretly, in disguise or under false pretense, seeks information with the intention of communicating it to the enemy.

The spy is punishable with death by hanging by the neck, whether or not he succeed in obtaining the information or in conveying it to the enemy.

Art. 89. If a citizen of the United States obtains information in a legitimate manner, and betrays it to the enemy, be he a military or civil officer, or a private citizen, he shall suffer death.

Art. 90. A traitor under the law of war, or a war-traitor, is a person in a place or district under Martial Law who, unauthorized by the military commander, gives information of any kind to the enemy, or holds intercourse with him.

Art.91. The war-traitor is always severely punished. If his offense consists in betraying to the enemy anything concerning the condition, safety, operations, or plans of the troops holding or occupying the place or district, his punishment is death.

Art. 92. If the citizen or subject of a country or place invaded or conquered gives information to his own government, from which he is separated by the hostile army, or to the army of his government, he is a war-traitor, and death is the penalty of his offense.

Art. 93. All armies in the field stand in need of guides, and impress them if they cannot obtain them otherwise.

Art. 94. No person having been forced by the enemy to serve as guide is punishable for having done so.

Art. 95. If a citizen of a hostile and invaded district voluntarily serves as a guide to the enemy, or offers to do so, he is deemed a war-traitor, and shall suffer death.

Art. 96. A citizen serving voluntarily as a guide against his own country commits treason, and will be dealt with according to the law of his country.

Art. 97. Guides, when it is clearly proved that they have misled intentionally, may be put to death.

Art. 98. An unauthorized or secret communication with the enemy is considered treasonable by the law of war.

Foreign residents in an invaded or occupied territory, or foreign visitors in the same, can claim no immunity from this law. They may communicate with foreign parts, or with the inhabitants of the hostile country, so far as the military authority permits, but no further. Instant expulsion from the occupied territory would be the very least punishment for the infraction of this rule.

Art. 99. A messenger carrying written dispatches or verbal messages from one portion of the army, or from a besieged place, to another portion of the same army, or its government, if armed, and in the uniform of his army, and if captured, while doing so, in the territory occupied by the enemy, is treated by the captor as a prisoner of war. If not in uniform, nor a soldier, the circumstances connected with his capture must determine the disposition that shall be made of him.

Art. 100. A messenger or agent who attempts to steal through the territory occupied by the enemy, to further, in any manner, the interests of the enemy, if captured, is not entitled to the privileges of the prisoner of war, and may be dealt with according to the circumstances of the case.

Art. 101. While deception in war is admitted as a just and necessary means of hostility, and is consistent with honorable warfare, the common law of war allows even capital punishment for clandestine or treacherous attempts to injure an enemy, because they are so dangerous, and it is difficult to guard against them.

Art. 102. The law of war, like the criminal law regarding other offenses, makes no difference on account of the difference of sexes, concerning the spy, the war-traitor, or the war-rebel.

Art. 103. Spies, war-traitors, and war-rebels are not exchanged according to the common law of war. The exchange of such persons would require a special cartel, authorized by the government, or, at a great distance from it, by the chief commander of the army in the field.

Art. 104. A successful spy or war-traitor, safely returned to his own army, and afterwards captured as an enemy, is not subject to punishment for his acts as a spy or war-traitor, but he may be held in closer custody as a person individually dangerous.

SECTION VI
Exchange of prisoners - Flags of truce - Flags of protection

Art. 105. Exchanges of prisoners take place - number for number - rank for rank wounded for wounded - with added condition for added condition - such, for instance, as not to serve for a certain period.

Art. 106. In exchanging prisoners of war, such numbers of persons of inferior rank may be substituted as an equivalent for one of superior rank as may be agreed upon by cartel, which requires the sanction of the government, or of the commander of the army in the field.

Art. 107. A prisoner of war is in honor bound truly to state to the captor his rank; and he is not to assume a lower rank than belongs to him, in order to cause a more advantageous exchange, nor a higher rank, for the purpose of obtaining better treatment.

Offenses to the contrary have been justly punished by the commanders of released prisoners, and may be good cause for refusing to release such prisoners.

Art. 108. The surplus number of prisoners of war remaining after an exchange has taken place is sometimes released either for the payment of a stipulated sum of money, or, in urgent cases, of provision, clothing, or other necessaries.

Such arrangement, however, requires the sanction of the highest authority.

Art. 109. The exchange of prisoners of war is an act of convenience to both belligerents. If no general cartel has been concluded, it cannot be demanded by either of them. No belligerent is obliged to exchange prisoners of war.

A cartel is voidable as soon as either party has violated it.

Art. 110. No exchange of prisoners shall be made except after complete capture, and after an accurate account of them, and a list of the captured officers, has been taken.

Art. 111. The bearer of a flag of truce cannot insist upon being admitted. He must always be admitted with great caution. Unnecessary frequency is carefully to be avoided.

Art. 112. If the bearer of a flag of truce offer himself during an engagement, he can be admitted as a very rare exception only. It is no breach of good faith to retain such flag of truce, if admitted during the engagement. Firing is not required to cease on the appearance of a flag of truce in battle.

Art. 113. If the bearer of a flag of truce, presenting himself during an engagement, is killed or wounded, it furnishes no ground of complaint whatever.

Art. 114. If it be discovered, and fairly proved, that a flag of truce has been abused for surreptitiously obtaining military knowledge, the bearer of the flag thus abusing his sacred character is deemed a spy.

So sacred is the character of a flag of truce, and so necessary is its sacredness, that while its abuse is an especially heinous offense, great caution is requisite, on the other hand, in convicting the bearer of a flag of truce as a spy.

Art. 115. It is customary to designate by certain flags (usually yellow) the hospitals in places which are shelled, so that the besieging enemy may avoid firing on them. The same has been done in battles, when hospitals are situated within the field of the engagement.

Art. 116. Honorable belligerents often request that the hospitals within the territory of the enemy may be designated, so that they may be spared. An honorable belligerent allows himself to be guided by flags or signals of protection as much as the contingencies and the necessities of the fight will permit.

Art. 117. It is justly considered an act of bad faith, of infamy or fiendishness, to deceive the enemy by flags of protection. Such act of bad faith may be good cause for refusing to respect such flags.

Art. 118. The besieging belligerent has sometimes requested the besieged to designate the buildings containing collections of works of art, scientific museums, astronomical observatories, or precious libraries, so that their destruction may be avoided as much as possible.

SECTION VII
Parole

Art. 119. Prisoners of war may be released from captivity by exchange, and, under certain circumstances, also by parole.

Art. 120. The term Parole designates the pledge of individual good faith and honor to do, or to omit doing, certain acts after he who gives his parole shall have been dismissed, wholly or partially, from the power of the captor.

Art. 121. The pledge of the parole is always an individual, but not a private act.

Art. 122. The parole applies chiefly to prisoners of war whom the captor allows to return to their country, or to live in greater freedom within the captor's country or territory, on conditions stated in the parole.

Art. 123. Release of prisoners of war by exchange is the general rule; release by parole is the exception.

Art. 124. Breaking the parole is punished with death when the person breaking the parole is captured again.

Accurate lists, therefore, of the paroled persons must be kept by the belligerents.

Art. 125. When paroles are given and received there must be an exchange of two written documents, in which the name and rank of the paroled individuals are accurately and truthfully stated.

Art. 126. Commissioned officers only are allowed to give their parole, and they can give it only with the permission of their superior, as long as a superior in rank is within reach.

Art. 127. No noncommissioned officer or private can give his parole except through an officer. Individual paroles not given through an officer are not only void, but subject the individuals giving them to the punishment of death as deserters. The only admissible exception is where individuals, properly separated from their commands, have suffered long confinement without the possibility of being paroled through an officer.

Art. 128. No paroling on the battlefield; no paroling of entire bodies of troops after a battle; and no dismissal of large numbers of prisoners, with a general declaration that they are paroled, is permitted, or of any value.

Art. 129. In capitulations for the surrender of strong places or fortified camps the commanding officer, in cases of urgent necessity, may agree that the troops under his command shall not fight again during the war, unless exchanged.

Art. 130. The usual pledge given in the parole is not to serve during the existing war, unless exchanged.

This pledge refers only to the active service in the field, against the paroling belligerent or his allies actively engaged in the same war. These cases of breaking the parole are patent acts, and can be visited with the punishment of death; but the pledge does not refer to internal service, such as recruiting or drilling the recruits, fortifying places not besieged, quelling civil commotions, fighting against belligerents unconnected with the paroling belligerents, or to civil or diplomatic service for which the paroled officer may be employed.

Art. 131. If the government does not approve of the parole, the paroled officer must return into captivity, and should the enemy refuse to receive him, he is free of his parole.

Art. 132. A belligerent government may declare, by a general order, whether it will allow paroling, and on what conditions it will allow it. Such order is communicated to the enemy.

Art. 133. No prisoner of war can be forced by the hostile government to parole himself, and no government is obliged to parole prisoners of war, or to parole all captured officers, if it paroles any. As the pledging of the parole is an individual act, so is paroling, on the other hand, an act of choice on the part of the belligerent.

Art. 134. The commander of an occupying army may require of the civil officers of the enemy, and of its citizens, any pledge he may consider necessary for the safety or security of his army, and upon their failure to give it he may arrest, confine, or detain them.

SECTION VIII
Armistice - Capitulation

Art. 135. An armistice is the cessation of active hostilities for a period agreed between belligerents. It must be agreed upon in writing, and duly ratified by the highest authorities of the contending parties.

Art. 136. If an armistice be declared, without conditions, it extends no further than to require a total cessation of hostilities along the front of both belligerents.

If conditions be agreed upon, they should be clearly expressed, and must be rigidly adhered to by both parties. If either party violates any express condition, the armistice may be declared null and void by the other.

Art. 137. An armistice may be general, and valid for all points and lines of the belligerents, or special, that is, referring to certain troops or certain localities only.

An armistice may be concluded for a definite time; or for an indefinite time, during which either belligerent may resume hostilities on giving the notice agreed upon to the other.

Art. 138. The motives which induce the one or the other belligerent to conclude an armistice, whether it be expected to be preliminary to a treaty of peace, or to prepare during the armistice for a more vigorous prosecution of the war, does in no way affect the character of the armistice itself.

Art. 139. An armistice is binding upon the belligerents from the day of the agreed commencement; but the officers of the armies are responsible from the day only when they receive official information of its existence.

Art. 140. Commanding officers have the right to conclude armistices binding on the district over which their command extends, but such armistice is subject to the ratification of the superior authority, and ceases so soon as it is made known to the enemy that the armistice is not ratified, even if a certain time for the elapsing between giving notice of cessation and the resumption of hostilities should have been stipulated for.

Art. 141. It is incumbent upon the contracting parties of an armistice to stipulate what intercourse of persons or traffic between the inhabitants of the territories occupied by the hostile armies shall be allowed, if any.

If nothing is stipulated the intercourse remains suspended, as during actual hostilities.

Art. 142. An armistice is not a partial or a temporary peace; it is only the suspension of military operations to the extent agreed upon by the parties.

Art. 143. When an armistice is concluded between a fortified place and the army besieging it, it is agreed by all the authorities on this subject that the besieger must cease all extension, perfection, or advance of his attacking works as much so as from attacks by main force.

But as there is a difference of opinion among martial jurists, whether the besieged have the right to repair breaches or to erect new works of defense within the place during an armistice, this point should be determined by express agreement between the parties.

Art. 144. So soon as a capitulation is signed, the capitulator has no right to demolish, destroy, or injure the works, arms, stores, or ammunition, in his possession, during the time which elapses between the signing and the execution of the capitulation, unless otherwise stipulated in the same.

Art. 145. When an armistice is clearly broken by one of the parties, the other party is released from all obligation to observe it.

Art. 146. Prisoners taken in the act of breaking an armistice must be treated as prisoners of war, the officer alone being responsible who gives the order for such a violation of an armistice. The highest authority of the belligerent aggrieved may demand redress for the infraction of an armistice.

Art. 147. Belligerents sometimes conclude an armistice while their plenipotentiaries are met to discuss the conditions of a treaty of peace; but plenipotentiaries may meet without a preliminary armistice; in the latter case, the war is carried on without any abatement.

SECTION IX
Assassination

Art. 148. The law of war does not allow proclaiming either an individual belonging to the hostile army, or a citizen, or a subject of the hostile government, an outlaw, who may be slain without trial by any captor, any more than the modern law of peace allows such intentional outlawry; on the contrary, it abhors such outrage. The sternest retaliation should follow the murder committed in consequence of such proclamation, made by whatever authority. Civilized nations look with horror upon offers of rewards for the assassination of enemies as relapses into barbarism.

SECTION X
Insurrection - Civil War - Rebellion

Art. 149. Insurrection is the rising of people in arms against their government, or a portion of it, or against one or more of its laws, or against an officer or officers of the government. It may be confined to mere armed resistance, or it may have greater ends in view.

Art. 150. Civil war is war between two or more portions of a country or state, each contending for the mastery of the whole, and each claiming to be the legitimate government. The term is also sometimes applied to war of rebellion, when the rebellious provinces or portions of the state are contiguous to those containing the seat of government.

Art. 151. The term rebellion is applied to an insurrection of large extent, and is usually a war between the legitimate government of a country and portions of provinces of the same who seek to throw off their allegiance to it and set up a government of their own.

Art. 152. When humanity induces the adoption of the rules of regular war to ward rebels, whether the adoption is partial or entire, it does in no way whatever imply a partial or complete acknowledgement of their government, if they have set up one, or of them, as an independent and sovereign power. Neutrals have no right to make the adoption of the rules of war by the assailed government toward rebels the ground of their own acknowledgment of the revolted people as an independent power.

Art. 153. Treating captured rebels as prisoners of war, exchanging them, concluding of cartels, capitulations, or other warlike agreements with them; addressing officers of a rebel army by the rank they may have in the same; accepting flags of truce; or, on the other hand, proclaiming Martial Law in their territory, or levying war-taxes or forced loans, or doing any other act sanctioned or demanded by the law and usages of public war between sovereign belligerents, neither proves nor establishes an acknowledgment of the rebellious people, or of the government which they may have erected, as a public or sovereign power. Nor does the adoption of the rules of war toward rebels imply an engagement with them extending beyond the limits of these rules. It is victory in the field that ends the strife and settles the future relations between the contending parties.

Art. 154. Treating, in the field, the rebellious enemy according to the law and usages of war has never prevented the legitimate government from trying the leaders of the rebellion or chief rebels for high treason, and from treating them accordingly, unless they are included in a general amnesty.

Art. 155. All enemies in regular war are divided into two general classes - that is to say, into combatants and noncombatants, or unarmed citizens of the hostile government.

The military commander of the legitimate government, in a war of rebellion, distinguishes between the loyal citizen in the revolted portion of the country and the disloyal citizen. The disloyal citizens may further be classified into those citizens known to sympathize with the rebellion without positively aiding it, and those who, without taking up arms, give positive aid and comfort to the rebellious enemy without being bodily forced thereto.

Art. 156. Common justice and plain expediency require that the military commander protect the manifestly loyal citizens, in revolted territories, against the hardships of the war as much as the common misfortune of all war admits.

The commander will throw the burden of the war, as much as lies within his power, on the disloyal citizens, of the revolted portion or province, subjecting them to a stricter police than the noncombatant enemies have to suffer in regular war; and if he deems it appropriate, or if his government demands of him that every citizen shall, by an oath of allegiance, or by some other manifest act, declare his fidelity to the legitimate government, he may expel, transfer, imprison, or fine the revolted citizens who refuse to pledge themselves anew as citizens obedient to the law and loyal to the government.

Whether it is expedient to do so, and whether reliance can be placed upon such oaths, the commander or his government have the right to decide.

Art. 157. Armed or unarmed resistance by citizens of the United States against the lawful movements of their troops is levying war against the United States, and is therefore treason.

Ava Lindsey Chambers

Dundury

What YOU, the Reader, thinks is important to us:

(Responders receive an "advance discounted" copy of Ava's next book)

1. <u>I bought the book because:</u>
   - ❏ the cover intrigued me
   - ❏ I heard Ava on a radio/tv talk show
   - ❏ the first pages hooked me

2. <u>I think Ava's writing is:</u>
   - ❏ okay
   - ❏ powerful--I couldn't put the book down
   - ❏ sensitive and compelling

3. <u>The story made me:</u>
   - ❏ SAD - because the characters were so real
   - ❏ THINK - that evil does take on so many different forms
   - ❏ MAD - that the "rules" of war had been set aside

4. <u>The book should:</u>
   - ❏ never have been written
   - ❏ be read by everyone because of its powerful message
   - ❏ be made into a movie

5. <u>I want to know:</u>
   - ❏ when Ava's next book is coming out
   - ❏ when Ava will be talking about her book on TV
   - ❏ when the book will be available on audiocassette or CD

6. <u>I will:</u>
   - ❏ tell my friends to buy this book
   - ❏ ask my library to order Ava's book
   - ❏ ask my local radio/tv talk show to interview Ava

NAME_____

ADDRESS_____

CITY_____STATE____ZIP_____

EMAIL_____

❏ Please put my name on FirstWorks' mailing list

❏ Send me an autographed copy of DUNDURY ($16.95)
(Plus GA 6% sales tax and $4.50 S/H)

❏ Check is enclosed (*please allow 3-4 weeks for delivery*)

❏ Money Order is enclosed

Return: FirstWorks Publishing Co., Inc. / PO Box 93
Marietta, GA 30061-0093

Ava Lindsey Chambers

Dundury

FirstWorks Upcoming Titles

SUGAR IN THE GOURD
by Ben Garrison

INTO THE TWILIGHT
Selected Short Stories & Southern Nights
by S.W. Lowery

BETRAYED
by Dani Dubre'

THE GRIFFIN GIRLS
A Sister Remembers
by Marge Glausier

DUNDURY (SEQUEL: YET TO BE TITLED)
by Ava Lindsey Chambers

Currently Available:

THE PALE HORSE COMETH
by Dani Dubre' & Rod Mauck

Ava Lindsey Chambers

Dundury

Ava Lindsey Chambers

Printed in the United States
18891LVS00002B/58-345